Jeanne Clair

# The
# Fifteen
# Houses

*A Novel*

outskirtspress

DENVER, COLORADO

The Fifteen Houses
A Novel
All Rights Reserved.
v4.0

Outskirts Press, Inc.
http://www.outskirtspress.com

ISBN: 978-1-4787-1849-9

Library of Congress Control Number: 2012918260

Outskirts Press and the "OP" logo are trademarks belonging to Outskirts Press, Inc.

PRINTED IN THE UNITED STATES OF AMERICA

To my beloved children, Ophelia and Scott,
The two greatest joys life sent my way.

# Author's Note

I loved developing the character of Julianne, the narrator of this novel, and the rest of the characters. I can relate deeply to the personal challenges that Julianne overcame and to the wonderfully complex level of depth in her character. I have a wealth of personal inspiration and memories that were interwoven throughout the novel and the demographic backdrop is also certainly personal as I used my hometown as a lovely setting for this story. Yet, despite some familiarities, this is a work of fiction. I have developed the *Fifteen Houses Series* of which this is the debut novel in the first person narration. I truly hope that you will enjoy reading every page as much as I enjoyed creating and molding every page.

# TABLE OF CONTENTS

# PROLOGUE
## *The Story House*

As a young woman in my twenties and thirties, I (Julianne) tried everything in my power to suppress in a vault within my brain, the collection of the memories of my younger days. During these years, I tried to focus on and relish in only the secondary part of my life. I created a kind of facade and acted as though only happier times ever existed. As I lived each day, I carried on as though my early Massachusetts existence had been only a series of recurring nightmares brought only to life in the middle of the quiet space of slumbered darkness.

Truthfully, it wasn't until much later in life that I saw how the dots of the life I had left behind and the life that I had formed for myself connected, and how the first part had a strong bearing on the latter. Whether I wanted those haunting memories to surface or not, they were indelibly connected as I have come to learn. The past forms you from tiny fibers and no matter how hard I may have tried to block flashbacks and those bad experiences out of the bright light surrounding my current happiness, it really isn't hard to see where traces of darkness have seeped through and clouded my character and actions in the paths I have chosen, and in the decisions I have made.

It wasn't until I began writing this bit of story down in my late sixties that I actually realized and began to clearly decipher where certain patterns and characteristics that I had developed stemmed from. Personality traits and fears that I had developed such as the terrible dread I have of moving, for example, that has plagued me like leprosy for decades. I had thought because I did not allow my past to overlap the boundary of my present that I was immune to the lasting impact that those experiences might have had on me. I laugh now as I read this manuscript over and over at the naivety of my thirties and forties and I can now assuredly conclude that my hatred of instability in habitat was a fear incision from the first half of my life and from the trauma of the first dwellings I had lived in. It turns out that my strong desire to remain in consistency is a direct result of those fifteen houses with all of the buried secrets and strife that resided in them, and that continues to reflect and form patterns within me today.

Notably until the venture of composing this book began, I had not realized the origin of all of my little paranoid phobias, mainly the terrifying fear I still have of all creepy crawling creatures and from being anywhere in their vicinity. So, in a way, delving into the nightmares of the past and confronting them, facing forward, so to speak, has been extremely cleansing and wonderfully liberating, taking my self-awareness to the highest level and helping me appreciate and tenderly guard with affection my journey from then, the beginning, to the person that I am today. The healing properties of putting things long locked away into the wide open are soul baring and soul strengthening. I highly recommend others who have endured traumas to confront their own nightmares straight forwardly and enjoy the resulting better dreams that the mind can extend to those who have the courage and faith to do so.

The Fifteen Houses is where my own innermost reflection begins.......

# CHAPTER ONE
## The Pale Yellow House

*H*ailing from the small mill town of Gardner, Massachusetts, my mother, Edith, and her seven older siblings came into the world in the early 1920's. Town life was peaceful, simple and, one might say, quite "Norman Rockwell-ish." This simplistic atmosphere soon changed, however, when my grandparents because of economic circumstances had to relocate the family to the contemporary confines of aggressive city life in bustling Springfield, Massachusetts.

Edith was, at the time, a young woman of fourteen and no one would argue that already she proudly wore her heritage: a blended mixture of German, French and Indian like a strutting, fanning peacock. A few years later as World War II was ending, Gerard, a young veteran who himself was of English, French and Indian ancestry, was introduced to the flaunting Edith by her older, already engaged sister, Martha. Edith was eager to spread her wings and leave her parents' home and so, she began taking long evening strolls with her new beau through the city park, and it wasn't long before

Gerard put a glimmer of a diamond on her left hand. Edith's father consented and within a few short months they held a small, humble, winter wedding ceremony with relatives surrounding them. Everyone present gave their blessings and wished the couple unending happiness and joy as they began their union together. Sadly, hidden underneath those generous offerings of blessings and the piles of lovely presents, Edith was secretly struggling with deep wounds, insecurities and resentments leaving her already spiteful at eighteen. Gerard, on the other hand, was a head-over-heels lovesick twenty-two year old who was too blinded by lustful youth and his own emotions to notice that anything was awry with his betrothed.

Gerard saw their future, as many young newlyweds often do, through optimistic and idyllic eyes. In Gerard's opinion, Edith was as close to perfection as an esteemed, accomplished young lady could possibly be. He was entranced by her artistic talent and thought she was as beautifully displayed as the delicate, graceful paintings she created. As they began their new living arrangement, this image was shattered as it became increasingly evident to Gerard that neither Edith's mother nor her expensive boarding school education had actually prepared her for the protocol of married life. To Gerard's dismay Edith did not know her way around the kitchen. She did not even know how to boil water, let alone manage all of the other essential, elementary basics that create a blissful home life. Gerard sadly would soon observe on top of this that

Edith did not possess the skills needed to raise any of the children they were soon to be blessed with.

On the flip side of this marital coin, Edith was not solely flawed in the domestic department and as their lives merged, she would likewise see that Gerard, too, was lacking a few of the necessary skills himself to success-fully play his role of husband. In addition to not being the responsible, mature husband he had promised to be when fathering children with Edith, Gerard would prove many times over that he was also not adequately qualified to play the role of "father." Their marriage was already off to a rocky start.

Reflecting back on the many stories my parents' shared with their children over the years about their marriage and its "Antarctica" atmosphere, I always wondered if it was because of some oppressive, dark secrets within her that Edith never allowed herself to openly explore "love" in its proper place and why she never could adapt to the role of a loving wife and doting mother. Perhaps, it was the terrible childhood scars that she later confessed to bearing along with naïve insecurities and vulnerabilities that she carried with her like oversized luggage, which contributed to her dislike of her husband's "manly" touch from the very beginning of their bonded union. Edith steered away from the "bedroom" at all costs and labored industriously in her paintings and other hobbies. She was clever to exception in creating a myriad of diversions that kept her distant from Gerard and from fulfilling her "womanly" duties.

These fragilities did not make her the "perfect" match for Gerard who was in the prime of his life with raging hormones. He longed for her love amongst his other needs. His heart throbbed and ached like an overfilled wine sack, ready to burst at the seams from an over-abundance of physical cravings and physical desires. The absence of her warmth and his unfulfilled emotional and physical needs caused great emptiness within him and, unbeknownst to Edith at the time, this lack of attention created a hazardous void in him that he would later seek to fill elsewhere.

Their first house was a small pale yellow abode they had built together in an established family oriented neighborhood. It would be in this house that I would begin my life's journey. Interestingly, this house would happen to be just around the corner from her parent's front door. Edith had the conveniences that come from being within an arm's reach of her mother's apron strings, but, as you can imagine, having in-law neighbors undoubtedly created some unnecessary tension for the newlyweds.

Edith's parents were old fashioned, educated, and terribly prideful. Although, they did not always approve of the choices Edith and my aunts and uncles made, they did, however, always feel free to voice their thoughts. Her parents were pleased that Edith had married young and relieved them of their financial and social responsibility. Yet, I am certain they wished she had chosen a more affluent suitor for herself. Edith should have already learned in her eighteen years of interaction with her parents that

they were not known for praising, encouraging or supporting their children's decisions, achievements or any
ambitions they might have had. They did not refrain
from letting Edith know that, in their eyes, she had not
exactly made a good choice when she married Gerard
and, therefore, she would forever be spiraling towards fail-
ure and doom. Silently, Edith begged and craved beyond
anything else in this world her parent's approval, but she
was always being turned away, leaving her disappointed,
bitter and angry knowing she would never have the satisfaction of shining in their eyes. This was no doubt a
contributing source of the spite she harbored.

So, with that being said, just a few unsatisfied months
into their marriage, Edith surprised her husband with the
news that she was pregnant. Unfortunately, because of
the physical requirements performed at work, the responsibilities of maintaining the home and the anxieties of
impending motherhood, Edith miscarried. Her mother-
in-law always felt that she lost the baby intentionally out
of spite as she really did not want to be a mother. In my
mother's defense, she would tell me many times later in
life that the miscarriage was not a "self-remedied abortion." Losing the baby had been caused by the physical
stress her job required of her. It appears to me that Edith
always carried this loss deep within her soul. Clearly, due
to Gerard's mother's harsh accusation about the reason
Edith lost the baby, it does not appear to me that Edith's
mother-in-law had a good opinion of her son's choice of
a marriage mate to begin with. It seems both sides of the

family felt their children could have married better.

My parents survived their disappointments and weathered the storms of winter until spring arrived, shedding evidence of new birth. Flowers were blossoming and the leaves on the trees surrounding their house were turning green and, by fall, Edith found herself pregnant again. It was the beginning of the next spring season that Louisa, my parent's first child, was born.

My mother repeatedly told the story over the decades of how, just moments after her newborn daughter came into the world, she would declare to her shock and to any nurse that stopped to congratulate her that the baby, her newborn, was "Ugly." She further claimed that because little Louisa's small face was all squishy from the delivery that her baby "looked like a monkey!" No doubt the nurses found this to be a horrid thought (as of course we all did when hearing the story more times than I care to remember) and were probably wondering amongst themselves just what kind of parent my mother was going to be. For sure, this was an early indication suggesting that during our lifetime, the love we would thrive to have from our mother would never come to be. Can you imagine thinking your newly born baby was ugly? What a way to welcome a newborn into the world. The delight my mother took in telling that story hundreds of times over the years was just disturbing to poor, sweet Louisa. (By the way, having seen many infant pictures of my sister, it was impossible for me to fathom how anyone would consider her anything but beautiful and priceless).

According to the photographs, my sister, Louisa, had large brown eyes and dark hair. When she got older and her hair grew longer, she had beautiful brown ringlets. Little did this precious infant know at the time of her birth what the future had in store for her? My brother Gabriel came along a year after Louisa, and I, Julianne Marguerite, would follow a year after him. I was the second girl, the third child. Our brother Alan was born two years after me.

Before my parents knew it, the living space was getting tight and the walls were closing in on us. The pale yellow house had become too small for our expanding family and soon we were moving away from the dirt roads that surrounded our home. On one hand, we were forlorn to be leaving our playmates and familiar surroundings, but, on the other hand, we were distancing ourselves from my grandparents and their leashes, criticisms, hidden agendas and unpleasant influences. Moving would be a double-edged sword for all of us.

I clearly remember moving day. It was in the early part of spring. My brother Alan was dressed in his yellow snow suit and we were both outside where snow was still piled in heaps around the perimeter of our house. I had been taking one last ride on our green lawn swing in front of the house. I let the crisp spring air calm me as I swayed back and forth. It felt as if I had been transported to the Cape coast and was enchanted by the waves rolling and out. Swinging had a soothing effect on my soul. And then, before I knew it, we had moved.

# CHAPTER TWO
## The Slightly Larger House
## (Part One)

Next, we found ourselves living in a slightly larger home with a two-car garage in the small, neighboring town of East Longmeadow, Massachusetts. Our new home was a light gray clapboard house accented with black shutters. It had cement walls on both sides of the garage, which served as a brace and prevented the landscaping from washing down to the driveway below when it rained.

The hollyhocks bloomed bright as they grew alongside the sides of the house and by the rather large barn we now owned. An array of pink and yellow blossoms remains vivid in my memory. The slightly larger 3-bedroom home was purchased with profit made from the sale of the pale yellow house. The house had been purchased with an underlying purpose in mind as we would later learn. My mother's sister, Martha, along with her family would be living with us while they made adjustments to economic challenges they were currently facing in their own lives.

The room above the garage ceiling, where the sparrows often nested and had families of their own, is the room my parents claimed for themselves as the master bedroom. There was a large living room outside their bedroom and a playroom adjacent to this room. The other two bedrooms were in the other half of the house. The lone bathroom had a claw-foot tub and the kitchen was just around the corner from the bathroom. Can you imagine having just one bathroom?

I was four years old at the time we moved and proudly, I was already washing and drying dishes. Even though I was doing a "big girl's job," to accomplish this task, I had to stand on a chair in front of the sink. At my young age, my arms were too short for me to be able to reach the water faucets. My short legs didn't help the situation either. A chair was provided, at least until I grew another foot taller!

At times, my mother would stand guard over me and inspect the dishes as I washed them. Any pieces, that did not pass my mother's "white-gloved inspection," she triumphantly put back in the dishwater for me to rewash. She would smack me on the back of my hands for each unclean dish she found while glaring at me disapprovingly.

Even though I did not like being scolded by my mother when I missed a "spot" every now and then, just feeling the soothing, coolness of the dishwater over my little hands took away any "sting" her words would leave behind. I loved seeing how after the dishes were done my fingertips would be all white and wrinkly. Somehow

I always found this transformation fascinating. It amazed me to see how in just a short time in the water, my fingers went from being "prunes" to "raisins." I opted for the opportunity to wash dishes over having to iron my father's white handkerchiefs on wash day or on any day I was given a choice to do so.

Gathering the chicken eggs and feeding the young bull we now owned would be some of the "new" chores my siblings and I were responsible for doing each day. Feeding the rabbits that were snuggled in their cages alongside the barn and feeding our dog would also be added to this list of chores. No video game time for us.

Near the rabbit cages were a heap of old red bricks and pieces of broken cement. These were remnants of something that was no longer there. Daddy-long-legs spent the day sunning themselves on these bricks before they returned each night to the feast that might be waiting for them in their webs.

A clothesline stood outside our back door. Once a week when my mother did the laundry, our newly washed clothing would hang embracing the fresh country air as they dried. A vegetable garden was sprouting beyond this and some barbed wire fencing is what separated our property from the cows grazing in the green meadows on the other side. A pigsty that held nests of hornets could be seen a short distance away from our back door. After seeing hornets flying around the pen, I did not have to be told to stay away from this area. It seemed that it did not matter how far I stayed away or how careful I would be, I still managed to get stung a few times over the years.

The long dirt driveway leading to our house was bordered by a line of asparagus that grew every spring. I strongly suggest that asparagus should be "cleaned" and "cooked" before ingested. Ugh! I can still remember the bitter taste left in my mouth after I had swallowed a raw bite. I had not anticipated such a horrible taste. I had expected this bite to be sweet. When it was not, I was very surprised. It served me right for taking something that wasn't mine, and without my neighbor's permission. These overlooked the neighbors surrounding our home and the yards where we eventually passed our time. The spiders, the low flying birds, the bees and hornets or the stories that Louisa would entertain us with when we camped in the darkness of the apple orchard would be just memories of "small" discomforts my siblings and I would face early on in our lives.

East Longmeadow was a small town where the trees outnumbered the population of people who lived there. It was here that the red foxes jumped in the fields as they chased their food, and where the deep purple grapes hung on the sides of the paved roads they lined. Morning glories wrapped their blue or white blossoms around the base of the mailbox that held the newspaper and mail delivered to our home each day. It was here where the tall pine trees dropped their sticky drops of sap on the pine cones that fell to the ground, and sometimes on the wooden picnic table where we ate our lunches in the warmth of the summer sun.

I have memories of my father with his wavy blonde hair standing on the back step, shining handsomely, dressed in his dark blue police uniform. His uniform shirt with crisply starched pleats distinctly stood at attention over his chest like a medal. It was in the early 1950's that I would remember three distinct things: him in his uniform, the long dirt driveway leading to our house, and the short stocky woman walking over the small stones and pebbles to our door wearing her dark coat and hat.

I did not know it then, but looking back, if my memory can be trusted, that was the beginning of the succession of unfolding events that would change who we were, and how people would view us over the years to come. It was also the beginning of the lies that were weaved into our little minds and souls about the growing relationship between this woman, her husband and my mother and father.

These untruths and unforeseen occurrences would eventually cause deep emotional scars and mold who we would later become. It marked the downfall of our family, as we knew it to be. It was the beginning of the thorns that would prevent my siblings and me from ever being able to capture the innocence and trust that "should" have held us together.

The memories of our days running through the fields, petting the smooth fur of the rabbits, or chasing the baby chicks as they scattered around the barn trying to get away for us as we tried to catch them would never be forgotten. Yet, these joys from this day onward would never be enough to heal the wounds we would come to experience.

We would never again be a "real" family, or measure up to the all-American, idealistic family as depicted on the "Leave it to Beaver Show" that was aired weekly on our black and white RCA television screen, which sat on the floor by the window in the living room. We certainly were not going to have the "white picket fence" family life while planning who we would become. The only way this could be "real" for our family would be in our dreams.

We had a rather large extended family, with lots of aunts, uncles and cousins to go around. Our family gatherings were a mixture of good food and spirits. Long walks into the woods looking for salamanders under the rotting tree limbs that had fallen to the ground or looking for blueberries often kept us children busy while the adults lingered. Occasionally, we stumbled upon burned out campfires we assumed were made by hobos as they rested for the night on their journeys passing through our woods.

The men sat at our yellow kitchen table playing card games while they smoked their cigars or cigarettes and quenched their thirst with alcohol. I can still remember the foul odor as they exhaled breaths of whiskey like fire from a dragon's mouth. As I hung around the table watching the men play their card games, I had often asked to have a tiny "sip" of my father's drink. Most times, he would just say "no" and would tell me to go away.

Once, though, I recall him winking his eye at my

grandfather, my mother's father, as he poured a very small amount of this same drink he had been drinking into a glass and offered some to me. He told me to pick up the little glass and instructed that "I drink it down fast!" Obeying his orders, I did just as he said. I put the little glass, (a shot glass by the way), to my lips and practically inhaled my drink.

Less than two seconds later, it felt as if I had just hit a brick wall. I was feeling nauseous. As I ran to the bathroom around the corner from the kitchen, I could hear the men laughing like fierce hyenas acting ridiculously like they were more like four sheets to the wind, than two. I was still feeling the golden liquid burning in my throat as I stood by the sink in a profound state of shock. A few more seconds had passed when my father appeared behind the bathroom door to see if I was okay. All the while, I could see him holding back his laughter.

I really wanted to cry, but I held back my tears. I did not want to give my father any satisfaction from knowing he "pulled a fast one" on me. Yet, as I stood by the bathroom sink, I could not believe my father would do something this mean to me. I made a mental note never to request "anything" from my father's glass again! This was a cruel prank on my father's part. Up until this day, I have steered almost completely away from using any alcohol in my life, even while at social functions. When I married later in life, I could not bring myself to sip the wine from the wine goblet as the priest offered me some as part of the marriage ceremony. I simply dipped the tip of my tongue into the red wine and passed the goblet on to my new husband.

While the men played their card games to pass the time, the women in the family kept busy changing diapers and preparing meals. They caught each other up on the latest news about their families as they sat in a circle working on their knitting projects. It seemed we were together a lot, especially during the time my mother's sister, Martha, and her husband, Eric and their children moved in with us. This, by the way, turned out to be another contributing factor for our moving into a larger home in the first place. This was to be just a temporary arrangement until they could get back on their feet. These days were memories of good times. Times when we were all getting along with one another.

It would not be long, though, before the walls of security and normalcy started cracking and changes were starting to take place all around us. Over time, one by one, relatives began dropping out of our cozy, family circle. If only that woman had never showed up at our home. Images of this woman coming up our driveway still linger behind in the shadows of my memory and haunt me. I knew back then this "presence" would change our lives.

I wish I didn't remember the image of her ascending the gravel driveway to our house, and then, perhaps, I would also not remember how this intimacy between the four adults began. Unfortunately, my ability to recollect is crystal clear. Gerard had become good friends with a fellow police officer, David. David, too, was an exceptionally handsome man, with dark hair and Irish good looks. He sported round wire rimmed glasses that magnified the gleam in his eyes as they settled on the bridge of his nose. The short stocky woman in the dark coat and hat belonged to "him."

Her name was Irene and she was his wife. They had a young son, Matthew, who mirrored the similarities of his father's features, removing any suspicions and gossip of him not being his biological child. Their second child, a young son Collin, was also an exact replica of his father. Collin, at this time, was in the playpen with my younger sister Aude, born number six a year after Chloe', sibling number five surprised us with her arrival. This meant I was five years and four months old at the beginning of the twisted relationship between Gerard, Edith, Irene and David.

My sisters and I shared a very large bedroom. Our room had two sets of bunks. I slept on one of the top bunks. I hated the top bunk! Mostly, I feared falling out of the bed and finding myself on the floor, which seemed miles away. During the nighttime, I often climbed down the little ladder at the foot of my bed taking my blanket and pillow with me. It was here "under" the bottom bunk where I would go to sleep. Secure, at peace and out of harm's way. This eliminated any harm that "could" come my way from a fall off the top bunk, since I was conveniently already on the floor!

My brothers Gabriel and Alan shared a double bed in the room just outside our bedroom. On weekends, after we had fallen asleep, it became common for us to feel the warmth of Irene and David's children nestled next to us in our beds.

All holiday celebrations became conjoined. We had to share "our" aunts, uncles and cousins with this awkward troupe addition. I never liked this idea and I always wondered why my parents invited them. It set the precedence for future events and gatherings and almost anything we would do thereafter. We no longer did anything as a single family unit. Everything we did now included these tag-a-longs.

During this time, Irene began sporting a very large top over her bulging stomach, and later that fall she had a baby boy, Christopher. This bundle of joy, however, did not resemble David, not even slightly, and, later in life, we would learn what was long suspected—that he was truly my half-brother, a son who belonged to "my" father. This explained why everyone (aunts, uncles, neighbors, etc.) always thought he and I were siblings and why Gerard, "my" father, was in the bedroom with Irene and not her husband David after delivery. Also, instead of going to "their" home post-birth, Irene and the newborn baby boy spent their time together in "my" parent's bedroom with Gerard admiring the baby as Irene openly bared her breast to nurse. I did NOT like seeing this.

A short time later, Irene bore yet another son, my half-brother, Hugh. I began to wonder how far this was going to go. How could my mother stand back and not do something about this? Why did she allow her husband to father "another" child with Irene? Even at my young age, something was not sitting right. What I was seeing, weighed deeply on my soul, as I knew something was wrong, very wrong!

The bouncing baby boy now joined the many who, in the past, had occupied the old wooden playpen. This cemented the family union; we were now "one." Our family circle, which entailed Gerard, Edith and my five siblings, now also included Irene, David, and their two children, and my two half-brothers and me. We were always together. Every weekend, we would be together behind the curtains that hung in the windows of the "slightly larger house" that we had moved to.

Although I resented Irene's presence and intrusion at our home, I was quick to appreciate that she loved to bake. She was always bringing brownies to our house when she came on the weekends. I will admit these brownies were very delicious. Our stomachs thoroughly enjoyed every bite. Sometimes, she would surprise us with chocolate chip cookies. She kept these fresh in large glass jars with metal lids and safe from the greedy hands of the children who surrounded them. When eating these treats, the sweetness made my dislike for Irene disappear but only for a few "sugar coated" moments.

Something always kept Edith busy. And now with another family to occupy her time, she was becoming less and less attentive to her own growing family. Her children, who craved her attention, would now have to share what little morsels they received with this counterpart family that my parents had allowed to invade our lives. So even though Irene's baked goods might have eased the hunger pains, they could not ease the emotional pain caused by the lack of maternal instinct from my own mother and father.

Relatives and neighbors often inquired curiously, as to "Why this family stayed at our home every weekend?" They also wanted to know, "Why we did everything with them?" Some even boldly asked, "if Irene, David and their children lived with us" and, of course, they wanted to know "if we were all brothers and sisters?" The townspeople no longer saw us as separate families. Onlookers now referred to us as "the people who lived in that house!"

We spoke French! Irene, David and their children did not speak French. They spoke not one word of it! I would tell myself repeatedly that they did "not" belong to us and we did "not" belong to them! I did not care what people were thinking!

The secrets of the wife swapping, the four-way affair, prevented us from establishing any real, open, honest friendships with our peers as we started our schooling. It was difficult trying to explain to our friends who Irene and David were or why they were always at our house. We were under the strictest instructions never to divulge our family business to anyone. It was less embarrassing to just keep our friends at an arm's length, and to keep our home life hidden behind the closed curtains.

At this period in time, I also did not feel that we had the emotional support from those in the neighborhood and the community that surrounded us. Like our friends, they too had their questions and concerns about what was going on inside our home. My parents were oblivious to the reality of the damage they were causing to themselves and to their children. It seemed everyone knew about this "secret affair." When we were out and about, whether walking to town or out riding our bikes, the people in town would stare and shamefully talk about us. The adults thought somehow they were committing this deception under complete discretion, but clearly these four adults lived in the land of denial!

It was rather imposing on my siblings and me to have these unwanted guests in our home. We eventually grew accustomed to their presence even though we did not like it. We were children and there was nothing we could do about it. Who could we tell that would have had the courage to confront them and make a difference? Most people who "wondered" about the wife-swapping simply closed their eyes. Some family members later confided that they wanted to act in our behalf but kept silent out of fear of upsetting the apple cart. They did not want to "rock the boat" as they let me know years later when I asked why they did not help us. Going to the teachers or the Clergy would not have helped either. Telling the truth would have made it more difficult for us. We too, would keep silent. We made the best of the situation. This was not the time period when children openly discussed or sought help for their problems!

Louisa, being the oldest of all ten siblings, took the lead in keeping us entertained and out of trouble. She was only eight years old, but she bore an enormous brunt of the responsibilities that belonged to the adults. Mostly, we would pass our time outdoors, out of sight and out of the minds of our parents. We left them alone so they could play their own games. They lived a life that really did not encompass interaction with us children unless it was out of absolute necessity.

I can still remember some of the common childhood games we played, like "Follow the Leader," "Red Rover," "Tag," "Simon Says," and a game we called, "Statues." Louisa could be creative and always managed to find something fun for us to do when we got bored of these routine games. She would take us hunting for rabbits, looking for snakes or we played hide and seek in the darkness of the night, followed by the game, "Monsters." (I hated the horror movies we were allowed to watch as they would give Louisa new ideas on how she could scare us. She was already creative enough)!

Louisa kept watch over us like an eagle. Seemingly, she always knew where we were, and would watch over us with her big brown eyes turning in every direction like a periscope in a submarine. Her talons were ready to claw at any villain that would dare set their eyes on us, and many times coming between us and our abuser. Like an eagle, Louisa was ready to swoop down to protect us if we needed her. She sought to protect us from the dangers we might encounter "outside," from the various forms of abuse that showed their ugly faces "inside" our house, and at times she protected us from "each other."

Louisa became like a shadow behind us. At every opportunity, she would come to our aide when we were in trouble with one of the adults. When we were being punished and sent to bed without supper, Louisa managed to save us a little something to eat from her own meager portion of food. Later, she would sneak the hidden food to us as we lay famished in our beds. This saved us from the hunger pangs that would be tormenting our little bodies. I don't know what we would have done without her constant care. Truly for me, the day Louisa was born turned out to be one of the most important days of our lives.

Moments like these and others like them generate memories of some of the tender acts Louisa expressed on our behalf. The adults who "should" have taken the lead had forfeited their responsibilities and just turned their heads. Louisa, a child herself, all too soon had the weight of the world on her shoulders. I never could quite figure out how she managed so well.

I suffered a great deal during this time in my childhood from respiratory and middle ear infections, which would eventually affect my hearing. I remember several times around the ages of six and seven that I had traveled a great distance to a large building that had many, many rooms. I did not know why I went there, or why my mother would leave me there. I do not remember my mother or father sitting me down, as a loving parent would, and explain to me why I needed to be at the hospital (as I later discovered was the name of the building). I do not recall my parents ever explaining what would be happening once they left me at the hospital. They just "left" me in the darkness of the night in this strange building out of their care. What I do remember, though, is being sick. This pain and the ear surgeries that followed would be a consistent trademark throughout my childhood, and continued to be right on into my adult years.

During one hospital stay, I was away from my home for two weeks and it seemed like an eternity. Louisa tried her best to ensure me of her love and found ways to let me know that she was thinking of me. We had few belongings. Still, Louisa sent her precious map puzzle with the little white pegs. I spent many hours at the hospital matching the proper "capitals" (the white pegs) with the "states" (the large white pieces).

During the long hours spent away from school while I was recuperating, Louisa and her classmates wrote cheerful letters and sent me best wishes for a speedy recovery. Louisa carried these letters home to me with great pride. She wanted me to know she cared. She was such a bright light around me.

My older brother Gabriel went to the hospital himself once, just after I had returned home. He had an infection in the lining of his heart. I was scared. I was afraid I wouldn't see my brother again. It was Christmastime.

Christmas morning came and went. We could not open our presents. They remained wrapped under the green boughs of the tree. The tree was decorated with liquid ornaments that reflected on the walls surrounding the tree as they shined their lights brightly. These lights would remain on until Gabriel returned home a few days later. Only then, could we open the treasures that were still wrapped beneath the tree. There was a tricycle, a cowboy hat, a gun and holster set, crayons, coloring books, paper dolls and candy canes. Somehow, the soothing effect of the peppermint candy canes as they were dissolving on my tongue made any discomfort I was feeling seem better. I had convinced myself that now Gabriel was safely home, everything would be okay.

During these hard times, Louisa was the strength that allowed us to hang on and endure the hours of mental and physical suffering. Her acts of kindness and caring would dwell forever in the hollows of my memory as I let go of the walls of anger I held within me in later years to come.

Warring within my own disquieting thoughts, I often wondered "when" it would be the right time for someone—anyone—to correct the men and women (mainly my parents) who brought children into this world and failed to show them the love they "should" have given them. I also wondered how my parents could allow individuals to come into their home and shatter what could have been, what should have been? I shamefully would wonder when discipline would be handed out to my parents who slacked in their responsibility to provide and nourish the emotional growth of their offspring. "When?" I would ask myself this question again and again, and then I would wait in silence for my answer. In my heart, I knew it was wrong to wish pain on someone else, but I could not help it. My pains and those of my siblings would fill luggage too heavy for us to carry. "When" continued to echo in my mind.

# CHAPTER THREE

## *The Slightly Larger House (Part Two)*

As a visual child, I learned to acutely become aware of the environment around me. For instance, I loved seeing evidence around our home letting me know that the fall season was about to begin. Things such as the big purple grapes hanging low to the ground at the end of our driveway while their leaves were turning a golden yellow or the cornstalks in the field that were heavy with ears of corn, ready and waiting to be picked. These were some of the noticeable signs alerting me that the summer season was ending and the new school year was about to begin.

Mixed emotions around my going back to school, kept my mind whirling with questions. What would my new classmates and teachers be like? Would they like me? Would I fit in? I was also hoping that I would not miss as much school because of illness as I had the previous school year. There was a touch of both nerves and excitement all intertwining together causing goose bumps to appear on my arms. On the last night of summer vacation, I drew my blanket up closer around my neck and eagerly waited for the morning sun to come up in the East, which would signal the start of the new day and the new school year.

My new socks were on the dresser with my old shoes, which I had polished earlier during the day. Irene had made me a dress with school books, apples, and ABC's printed all over it. As I stared at the new dress hanging on the outside of the closet door, I could see the blue in the dress appearing to change color as the room began to darken. The dress had a purple hue and I imagined that the big yellow letters were stars in the shape of different letters of the alphabet. I must say, I had quite an imagination!

In the mornings, my sister Louisa, my brother Gabriel and I would walk to our bus stop. I recently went back to this house and measured the distance from the bus stop to the end of our driveway. It was exactly one mile (not the seven that I had always told my children it was). It did not matter what the weather was like outside the windows of our home. There were no other alternatives for us. My father had taken the only car we owned when he left earlier in the morning for work. Louisa's eight year old legs, Gabriel's seven year old legs and my six year old legs would have to walk speedily if we wanted to catch the bus. That mile certainly felt like seven million instead of the seven miles I thought it was!

To add to the stresses of Louisa's already heavy burden, most times we left the house without the necessary funds to pay for our bus fare. It was humiliating and a little challenging to try and get on the bus without money as you can easily imagine! Many mornings we boarded the bus with our faces glowing BRIGHT red from embarrassment. How it worked was, Louisa would motion for us to go sit down as she distracted the bus driver while pretending to put the appropriate change in the coin slot. More often than not, the bus drivers took pity on us and let us get on without fare. The bus would then take us about six miles away to the fancy French School we attended. At least once, my sister Louisa recalls, for some reason the bus driver didn't look the other way and, let's just say, it was a long, long walk home only to be met by our mother wondering why in the world we were home so soon.

I could not understand why my parents did not provide us with the proper funding for the bus fare. If we could not afford the transportation cost, why did we continue going to the French School? Instead, why didn't my parents send us to a "free" Public School? It did not make sense.

In the afternoon, the bus would bring us back to where it had picked us up earlier that day. We would then walk the one mile back to our home. In the rain, the sleet and the snow, we would walk, just like the mail carrier. It did not harm us to walk to the bus stop. In fact, our mother often reminded us that the "fresh air would be good for us!" As we walked, any grasshoppers left over from the summer would show themselves now and then. I did not love these hopping bugs. I did not mind them, though, as long as they did not jump on me!

A short distance down the road from our house there was a small brook. In the spring, we would collect polly-wogs and keep them in jars only to have to return them to the brook before they died in our care. These were our mother's orders!

Still, we went to the brook several times a day to check on their progress. Like little biologists, we documented in our minds their changes as they appeared before our eyes. We observed them as they grew their tails. Eventually legs would appear on their bodies. We watched them as they would swim around in the water. They were fast like Olympic swimmers, as they darted in and out between the undergrowth that was sheltering them.

In the summertime, flowers would cover the field by the brook. There were light purple flowers that seemed almost white until you got up close to them. Dandelions were among my favorite flowers that grew in the field, which, of course, are actually weeds. Eventually, we could blow the seeds off the stems when the blossoms shed their colors. I loved watching the seeds fly in the air until they landed on the soft ground where they might sprout the following spring. Later in the fall, the milkweed pods would split open and these, too, would send their long silky seeds flying all around us.

Where we crossed the street at the four-way stop, this marked the halfway point to our bus stop. It was on this side of the road that was home to the biggest apple orchard my eyes had ever seen. Once, when walking by on our way home from school, the people picking apples offered some to us. We took them home and showed our mother the nice big delicious treats someone had just given us. Free!

After explaining the dangers of taking something from people we did not know, we were made to promise not to do the same again. Our mother then screened the apples to make sure that there were no "razors" hidden under the skins and that they were safe for us to eat. Seriously? When she ensured us the apples were okay, we washed and shined them before taking our first bite. Crunch. Yummy. This was a real treat for us as we would be hungry after a long day at school. These apples gave us something to eat that would ward off our hunger pangs as we awaited our supper meal that night.

I did not like going to school, but I did enjoy the time I shared the same class with my cousin, Marie Ann. We were just about the same age, give or take a month or two (five months to be exact). Marie Ann had long brown hair with bouncing ringlets just like my sister Louisa. What I did not like about being classmates with Marie Ann was that she told her mother, my Aunt Martha, everything I did, right or wrong. My Aunt Martha then called my mother and let her know what I had done. This was not always a good thing for me as there were times I did get in my share of trouble. Early on in my life, the shrill of the telephone ringing in our house sent me running to hide in my bedroom closet especially when I knew I had misbehaved at school.

The nuns would tape my gum to my nose when I had been caught chewing in class. Another time, I had gotten in trouble for crawling under my desk to retrieve the pencil I had dropped. More trouble came my way when I was using my textbook during a test to check on the spelling of a word I needed to write. The nun had seen me and marched right up to my desk and placed a big fat "red" zero at the top of my page! Either I had not been discreet when removing my book from the belly of my desk to make sure no one saw me, or the nun had eyes in the back of her head just like my mother did! I truly believe it was the latter of the two choices. The nun had eyes in the back of her head. I am sure of it!

My teacher, dressed in her black "habit" and with a white "halo" around her face, did not have any difficulty enforcing strict discipline. I can still remember Joseph being brought up to the front of the class and placed over the nun's lap as she applied the ruler to his pink bottom. I would never forget this boy's face, even as time went by, because of this incident. Still, it was not enough to keep me from finding trouble.

Once in the schoolyard, I was playing the game, "Get out Of My Way before I Kick You." This was a very popular schoolyard game in the 1950's. When I played this game, I did not care who was in front of me. If you did not get out of my way, you received a kick in the pants. That was the rule! On this particular day, however, I should have bent the rules some and allowed the nun in front of me some slack instead of kicking her. I may still have had all the buttons on my coat when I returned home from school later that day. Four little pink buttons popped right off my coat as I hung in the air as the nun gripped me by the collar of my coat. To make matters worse, I had a cousin and a sister who raced home to be the first to tell my mother how the buttons happened to be in my hand and not on my coat.

One time, our class had a part in a school play about the Alphabet. The Alphabet was sung in French, which I might add I can proudly still sing! I wore a costume that looked like a pair of pajamas. The fancy top had black loops that wrapped themselves around the buttons. Even though we had to give the costume back after the play, it was nice to be wearing something new even if it was for a little while. On the way to the play, my mother had stopped at the police station so I could show David my outfit. I did not understand why we had gone to see him and not my father. I do remember my mother smiling as she flirted with David as he sat behind the office desk. I did not like the way my mother smiled at David. I did not like the way David smiled back at my mother. Icky, queasy feelings, ugh! This took away any joy I had gleaned from wearing the costume. I was now feeling shame as I knew they were doing something wrong! They couldn't hide their mischievousness, and secrecy was written all over their faces.

In the fall during recess, we collected leaves as they were scattered around us on the playground. We looked for the brightest and prettiest leaves we could find.

After recess was over, we brought our autumn treasures into the warmth of our classroom. With pride, we displayed these treasures on our desks. Later, when our schoolwork was completed, we traced these leaves on paper and colored them. Other times, we then pasted them on colorful paper and then we would hang them on the big windows in our classroom so everyone on the outside of the classroom could see them.

One bad thing about the fall season ending was that winter was sure to follow. I did not like walking in the snow. There were times we would be very cold. This was not any fun for us. So that we would not freeze, Louisa kept us warm by keeping us moving. She had us walking around in circles or we jumped up and down. There were times she held our hands or put our hands in her coat pockets as we walked or waited for the bus to keep them warm. Our mother did knit us each a new pair of mittens every year; however, if you were careless and lost them, there would not be another pair to wear—not right away. Even though I did my best to keep track of these precious mittens, somehow, I lost one of mine down by the brook. I for one appreciated Louisa's warm hands and her willingness to keep mine from freezing.

Every morning, I had to kneel to recite my prayers for my mother in the doorway of the kitchen. My mother would listen as she scurried about getting breakfast together for us to eat after we finished our prayers. When I could not recite my prayers properly, my mother would often slap me across the head and make me repeat the prayers until I got them right. More than once, I was sent to school without my breakfast of burnt toast or some kind of disgusting oatmeal that would make me want to vomit when swallowed. Time went by so fast that many times I headed out the door before getting a chance to eat breakfast. My mother spent most of the time chastising me for not being able to say my prayers correctly in French. I also did not have the proper emphasis on the tongue rolling "R." I never did master this tongue rolling thing.

I did not understand why I hadn't repeated my prayers as correctly as my siblings had, when it had been their turn to recite their prayers. Seeing my brother eating his second bowl of cereal made my stomach growl covetously even more. I would try even harder as I was so hungry. I had trouble succeeding in this department. I often wondered if I was stupid. I couldn't say these prayers to my mother's expectations no matter how hard I tried. Years later, I came to understand that my problem had nothing to do with learning difficulties, but it was because I had not actually heard all the words needing to be repeated. How could I repeat words I did not hear? Why couldn't my mother understand this?

In the spring, I was not able to make my First Communion with my classmates. I could not hear the priest when I was in the Confessional Booth. I was still not able to hear him when he had me kneel before him on his side of the booth. The teachers felt that since I had not been able to hear the priest, I certainly did not hear their instructions leading up to this important step. They held me back from joining my classmates as they received this earned privilege.

I was devastated and feared returning home that night from school. I knew this situation was going to be a topic of conversation. I did not like being the center of attention. At this moment, I was feeling I had not made my parents proud. I kept my eyes cast downward so I wouldn't see the anger and disappointment in their eyes. I did not want to have to talk about this situation. I already felt bad enough and from this moment on, I knew I was different.

Shortly thereafter, we stopped going to the French School and we started to attend an English Public School closer to our home. This change in schools took place towards the end of the year when I was in second grade. Even though I was afraid to be starting over in a new school, I did like the fact that we would be taking a yellow school bus and that our new bus stop was at the end of our driveway. We no longer had to walk the mile to the other bus stop in the rain, sleet or snow. And, it was FREE! What a bargain.

Summer vacation from school had started and, soon after, my father's mother and his stepbrother came to visit us. I had not remembered seeing much of either of them before this visit. When my grandmother ended her visit with us, my step-uncle Gordon remained behind. Gordon spent many weeks with us. He slept in the tool room in the back of our big barn.

I can still remember how Gordon would tease Louisa. He would take her doll away from her and he wouldn't give it back. She begged him to give her back her doll. The doll was dressed in a bride's dress and it was special to Louisa. At this particular time, Gordon was violently swinging the doll around by its long black, braided hair. I was afraid Gordon would destroy the doll and that Louisa would not be able to play with her ever again. The more Louisa tried to make Gordon stop, the more he would swing the doll in the air. Higher and higher, out of her reach. Louisa did not like his actions and neither did I.

Later that night, my parents were going somewhere with the stocky woman and her husband. They left us in Gordon's charge. There was a small bag of lollipops on the maple coffee table in the living room. Gordon promised to give me this whole bag if I would play a game with him. Of course, I said YES! What child would have said NO? Gordon motioned for me to follow him into the bathroom. My brother Gabriel had also come into the bathroom with us. Gordon then shut the bathroom door and locked it.

My step-uncle picked me up and placed me on the toilet. He told me to close my eyes tightly and instructed me not to open them until he said I could do so. I obeyed him. I wanted the lollipops. I wanted to share them with my brothers and sisters. I did not know what Gordon was doing to me, but he was hurting me. He had separated my legs and was gripping them tightly with his hands to keep me from being able to move them away. I screamed for him to stop. I started to cry. Finally, he did stop and then he let go of my legs. He reminded me NOT to tell anyone what he had done.

At six years old, I do not believe I knew what he had done to me. What I did know, was that he hurt me and that he had put "something" where it did not belong. My heart raced; my ears were making funny noises and I felt sick to my stomach. Yet, I never did tell anyone. I also never received the bag of lollipops Gordon had promised me. That bag of lollipops sat on the coffee table unopened all night. I felt very sad that Gordon had hurt me but I was even more upset that he had lied to me. In all the years since that night, I never heard my brother Gabriel discuss this event or acknowledge to me what he had seen. It remains our secret.

After this incident, I kept my distance from my step-uncle. I did not let him get close to me again. I was afraid that he might hurt me and I avoided him at every oppor-tunity. Not long thereafter, he was gone. I never wanted to see him again.

I had spent many hours in silence, rehashing my pain and trying to make sense of what Gordon had done to me. I was young, I did not understand and I was ashamed. Immediately, I did notice changes that would come over me. I began to be afraid when left alone in the dark. For a long time, the memories of this pain followed me every time I had to use the bathroom. I hated taking off my undergarments. Over fifty years later, I still have panic attacks when I am asked to remove my clothing in a doctor's office for exams. After the doctors leave the room, big huge teardrops escape the dams inside my eyes that had been held back all these years.

Soon after this night, summer vacation came to an end. I could not wait for the new school year to start. Even though I did not actually enjoy school, going to school became a "safe haven for me." I wanted to be away from my house and the bad memories that were already starting to accumulate in my mind.

My new classroom was on the second floor of an old school that sat on top of a hill. Irene, David and their children lived at the bottom of the school hill. One day, I missed the bus that should have taken me home. I had to walk down the hill to the stocky woman's house so I could get a ride home. My father was already at Irene's house for some reason. He and Irene questioned me, to see why I had missed my bus. My father was sitting at the chocolate brown kitchen table with the green design on the borders that held the ashtrays where he would rest his cigarettes as he sat there talking with Irene. After my father took me home, my mother wanted to know why I missed the bus and the questioning started all over again.

I really believe that all the questions were to distract me from the underlying problem they really believed the world was oblivious to. Yikes! I had caught my father with Irene. He should not have been visiting with Irene. Why wasn't he at work? Where was David? Where was my mother? I am pretty sure that all the excitement over my missing the bus was to take the heat off them. Nothing more was ever mentioned around this incident.

On the weekends, our mothers allowed us to eat our supper in the living room as we watched the shows that came on during our meals. I can still recall morals learned from some of these shows today. 'The Lone Ranger', 'Sky King', 'Rin Tin Tin', 'The Roy Rogers Show', and 'Lassie', were just a few of the television programs we would view on Saturday nights. Every Saturday night, we ate our beans and hot dogs as we sat on the long maple couch with the floral slipcover watching TV.

I don't know what got this routine started, but, I absolutely hated beans. I could not bear to sink my teeth into the beans and chewing them was completely out of the question. Therefore, I would drop the beans (by the spoonful) behind the couch when no one was watching. My heart would pound, as I knew I would be in big trouble if I had been caught. Happily, our dog, Lady, received these "special treats" and ate any evidence I left behind. Lady was a good dog! Lady was my hero, my 'Lassie'.

In the summertime, we ate some of our meals under the shade of the pine trees on our wooden picnic table. I can still taste the freshly squeezed glasses of lemonade that my mother would make. I remembered how the lemonade made my lips pucker. We drank this lemonade from our, 'Bugs Bunny' or 'Tweety Bird and Sylvester the Cat' glasses. These logo pictured glasses were the selling pitch that made you want to buy the jelly that was inside. When the jelly was gone, these containers became our newest drinking glasses.

I loved the green grass that grew around our house. The grass was thick, yet it felt as smooth as a carpet. There was a hill to the right side of our house. We spent hours tumbling down this hill. We repeatedly rolled our bodies down the hill on the silky grass that covered the mound of dirt beneath us. We laughed as we rolled into each other. I can still smell the moist grass that grew among the pink and white clovers that tickled our skin as we would lay there when we stopped rolling. Then, we would stare at the moving clouds above us. We spent hours imagining what shapes the clouds were forming and counting the seconds it took for them to pass us by.

Summer showers meant we could run outside clad only in our underwear, and let the cool raindrops fall on our bodies. I don't think we owned bathing suits. While running about, we would try to catch the heavenly raindrops with our tongues as they fell all around us.

There were times when lightning and thunder would cut these special afternoons short as we would have to retreat inside taking away any chance of our being struck by the bolts of light that flashed in the sky or on the ground around us. I can clearly remember seeing my mother in the windows of the living room, counting the seconds between the flashing light and the noise that came with the crashing thunder. This let my mother know how close the storm was to our area. She did this every time we had thunderstorms so being young, I would imagine, this was an important task to be done during these storms. I made a mental note of this and stored it in my memory bank under the heading of: "things people did that I did not quite understand!"

Sadly, my mother and most of my siblings still become ridiculously afraid during thunderstorms. They will cancel all plans or appointments that they might have on any days the sky shows any hint of rain. They will not talk on the phone or make phone calls during thunderstorms for fear lightning might strike them dead. And, I still hear them count the seconds between the flashing lights and the sound of the thunder (one Mississippi, two Mississippi, three Mississippi...).

Puddles left behind from the rainstorms became temporary outlets of fun for our creative minds. Sometimes, we would wade barefoot in the freshly made puddles. I liked how the soft cool mud felt underneath my feet and all squishy between the toes. I also remembered adding foliage and dirt to these puddles to make some kind of potent "brew" and had it ready to feed any "monsters" that might come our way after these storms.

Mainly, I enjoyed the freshness in the air after the rain had cleansed the sky of the dark and dirty clouds. Blue sky would appear again. It seemed there was always a bird or two gracefully flying in the sky above. Everything had come back to normal. However, someone would always come around to spoil the beautiful pictures my mind would paint. Peaceful moments like these were short lived.

One afternoon, right after the new school year had started, Louisa and her neighborhood friend, Anne, had gone to the brook and decided that they were going to light some cattails that were drying by the water's edge. These lit cattails could then become their "torches." Louisa had obtained the matches from our brother Gabriel as he had just conveniently finished burning our daily trash in the rusted barrel outside by the big barn, and still had matches in his pockets. Louisa and Anne collected the cattails and put them in a pile. Oh dear.

The fall wind was blowing, naturally. The cattails ("torches") were burning nicely until the wind decided to blow some of the amber coals and consequently cause the field around them to catch on fire. Brilliant! Louisa ran home as fast as she could and told my mother about the fire. She did not need to go into some long explanation for my mother to understand her. She got directly to the point..."FIRE!" My mother then called the fire department. The image of the firefighter holding Louisa's "little red riding hood coat" smoldering on the tail end of a stick lingered in my mind for a long time. The fire destroyed the beautiful coat someone had just given my mother for Louisa to wear. The blue parka coat with its hood lined with red material was thrown in the trash. This was not good.

The "hoodlums" were in trouble, but not in as much trouble as their fathers were. Their children burned a grazing field that did not belong to them and the farmer had to be compensated for this loss. Anne's father and my father were both on the police force. Anne's father had recently been appointed a "safety officer" for our town. The fire was not going to make either of these fathers look good. It would not be good for Louisa, or for Anne. Unfortunately, so that they would remember to never to play with matches again or burn cattails, they were punished.

As time went passing by, I was missing my family, the original entity of the intact unit. I missed doing things with my own family. My mother's parents did not come around to play cards anymore. Irene was as unpleasant and as controlling as my own mother. Irene dominated the other three adults and most of the time called the shots. I did not like this. I'd wager a guess that my siblings did not like this either.

Towards the end of the school year, I came home from school and found my mother sobbing hysterically. My renegade father had the nerve to actually go and run off with the stocky woman. My mother was not sure if my father was going to come back. She was like a "deer in the headlights." He just left us! He left us without money for food or bills not to mention for the mortgage. He left without saying goodbye. However, he left something behind for my mother…David. Ugh! That was more of a liability than a grand going-away present.

My father was only gone one month (might have been better, in retrospect if he hadn't returned), but to me it seemed he had been gone a lifetime. When he did return, my mother cried even more. Her life was as mixed up as a bowl of tossed salad. She had made such a mess out of her life by allowing that stocky woman to come into her home. So much had rapidly transpired during the time my father was away. My mother could not carry the mortgage and six children, (no doubt they were already very behind on the loan and no doubt every other bill). No one from the family came with the glass slipper to help secure our needs. The loans she took from our little neighborhood friends didn't go far. How embarrassing to think she borrowed money from our friends. And David, her uniformed, lover, catch of the year, definitely didn't have a penny to his name. So, the bank took back the house we were living in. Thanks to the latest escapade we had lost our home. We had to move again. It was a sad time for all of us. However, maybe, just maybe, moving would give us a fresh start.

# CHAPTER FOUR

## The White House On Top of the Hill (Part One)

We were moving! I was hoping this meant we could go back to being our own family again. A family who would not get involved with any more of the drama connected with Irene, David and their children. Don't get me wrong. I did not harbor any resentment against their children. They were in for the long haul in this mess just as I was. They couldn't change any of it either. Ten children, (six children belonged to Gerard and Edith - two children belonged to David and Irene - two children belonged to Gerard and Irene). It was getting hard, trying to keep everyone's biological origin straight! All of us children were innocent victims, and we were all trapped by the crippling effects of this "secret affair."

While my father was in Florida with Irene and her children, he had decided after a month, that he was missing his own children and came back to Massachusetts to be with us. Unfortunately, Irene came back with him, and so did her children, and they were now back living with David. Once things around the home began to settle down some, my father started working his new job as a truck driver. He had lost his job working for the Police Department when he took off with Irene to Florida. Now, suddenly, changes were happening all around us. Again! I did not like changes.

We were now staring at the boxes stacked up in the bedrooms where we would sleep at night. While we were unpacking our belongings, we tried to accept that we were in a new house, and these were our new bedrooms. Moving weighed heavily on my soul, and I now had new emotions with which to struggle. Uprooted, just as quickly as the snap of a finger, I found myself in unfamiliar surroundings. Many questions flowed through my brain about the relationship my parents had with Irene and David. I knew better than to expose these questions to the lips that wished to ask them.

I had just turned eight years old a few months before this move. Even though I was getting older, moving had never been an enjoyable event for me. Does anyone really enjoy the process of moving? It was frightful to be leaving behind glimpses of memories from each of the houses I had lived in. In this case, however, I was happy to be leaving the slightly larger house to some degree. Moving would take me away from the place where my step-uncle had done bad things to me. This thought helped me readily accept the changes that came with moving again, and I began to uphold the general delusions of a fresh start. I also began to convince myself that my parents were thinking along the same lines. I know my other siblings were. Maybe Irene and David's children also hoped when we moved, they, too, could go back to enjoying their family without any interference from our end.

Shortly after my step-uncle had gone back home after his vacation with us, I heard from information gleaned from my parent's conversations that he was sent to jail for doing similar misdeeds he had done to me with another girl who was sixteen. At this time, the laws of the state considered this girl a minor. Police arrested Gordon after he had taken her, without her parents' consent, across the state line. I was thrilled to learn Gordon would not be coming to our house for a long time.

Tears were for babies so I held mine back. I did not want anyone to see me cry. I didn't want my parents or siblings thinking I was weak, sad, or afraid. Often, I hid within the walls of the closet in my bedroom to ensure that I would not draw attention to myself. I did not want anyone to know how I was really feeling. This way, they couldn't tease me or laugh at me. At times, I would linger a bit in the darkness of my closet, so that any redness around my eyes would disappear before I ventured out, hiding any evidence that tears had been shed. I always felt people could see through me, and that they knew what I was thinking. Being in the closet was like having a "fort" around my body. I had already experienced a few situations in my life that left me unhappy, and I did not need to add any more emotional woes to this list. If I was feeling the need for some personal space, the bedroom closet was a good place for me to retreat.

When I looked into the eyes of others around me, I felt they could read my mind. It would not have been a good idea for them to know what I was thinking, as often I was thinking of hurting myself, running far, far away, or how I could commit a perfect crime and get away with it. Sometimes, I had contemplated all three of these ideas at once. No one could penetrate the closet and guess my innermost thoughts. First of all, they had to find me. Secondly, they would need a flashlight to see me in the dark dungeon. By the time they found the flashlight, I would be done releasing my emotions, and no one would ever know what I was doing in the closet in the first place. I am sure, though, that no one ever even noticed the absence of my presence.

Although the closet afforded me a place to hide and release my anger or tears, it did not provide me with actual solutions to my problems. Problems continued to come my way. It was apparent that the stocky woman, her husband and their children were like an infection that would not go away. They had followed us to the new home. The weekend visits and their presence during celebrations would continue. They did not leave us alone. They had not gone away. They followed my family seven miles east to the white house on the top of the hill.

Our new home was old. It did not look like the newer homes going up around us in the neighborhood. My sister Louisa and I shared the bedroom facing the front side of the house. My sisters Aude and Chloe' slept in the bedroom across the hall from us. My brothers Gabriel and Alan had the bedroom to our left, just outside the bathroom. My mother had her bedroom down the hall from us for a short time and my father had his bedroom downstairs. After my sister Mildred was born, our bedrooms were switched. Aude and Chloe' moved into my mother's bedroom. Mildred now had the smaller bedroom they had previously occupied. The playroom downstairs would now become my mother's new bedroom.

The rented house had many rooms. There were six bedrooms, a kitchen, a dining room, a large living room, and a hall that would lead you to the front entrance of the house. It was in this hallway where the antique oak coat hanger, with bench and mirror, stood. Near the other end of this same hall, on the left by the door's frame leading into the kitchen, was an old Victrola (a.k.a. gramophone) sitting on an old table. Also, on this table, were a metal hand crank and a box of old albums. Short, fat, pointed needles were scattered about, either on the table or in the box. All these tools were needed and helped the Victrola to play its music.

Sounds flowed through the beautiful brass shaped horn and out into the world of ears that would listen. I loved listening to the albums, even though I did not understand any of the words of these Italian opera masterpieces. I longed to be part of the beauty that belonged to the peace and comfort I received from listening to the music, long after the records had stopped. Later, while the adults would scream and hiss, I could replay that comforting music in my head.

Against the wall opposite the Victrola was a black piano, another precious gem. It was sturdy and very heavy. This was probably the reason someone had left it behind when they moved away from the house, and no doubt the reason it would stay long after us. The notes that rang out when striking its keys, gave evidence, even to me, that the piano needed to be tuned. I did not care. I loved to touch the black and white keys. Up and down the keyboard, I would run my fingers. Doing this was more of an aggravation to those around me in the house, but, I didn't care. Toying with the piano helped erase the cares of my day. It took me on a carefree ride where I would float away into a world of music. When striking each key, I listened to the beautiful music I imagined I was making.

A bench was tucked under the piano near the metal foot petals. This bench held aging books and sheets of music; music I never learned to play. I did not know how to read music. Yet, I imagined that someone knew how to play these beautiful tunes. In their heart, somewhere, they may have been basking in the memories of glorious, musical days gone by. The piano and the Victrola, together, side by side. Yes, it was wonderful being able to roam about in my imagination.

Our new house was old, and stood out amongst the other houses on our established street. It dated back to the days of the American Revolution, when Indians still had settlements not too far away from our home.

The old dairy farm on one side of the house, still had paper-thin shacks where the farmhands, at one time, laid their tired bodies down when the sun set after a long day of work. The black and white cows were scattered about as they grazed in the overgrown bushes around these shacks behind our home that was a remnant of a pasture that used to be. Like the cows, my siblings and I often fended for ourselves. There were no farmers or farmhands to guide us. We would only have each other.

A clothesline ran from a post closer to our driveway and strung across the grass to the plum tree where a path had been made over the years by those who hung their wash to dry. We spent many summers under the tents we made hanging from this clothesline, with the clothespins securing the green army blankets that would shelter us on the nights we slept in these tents.

There was always a tent for the boys and one for the girls. Louisa would take us into the night with jars in our hands, to collect the lights that blinked on and off in the darkness around us. I loved how these fireflies blinked in the tent when we would set them "free" to fly around us, as Louisa told made up stories that left one believing might actually be true. She made the characters come so alive. Louisa could make you feel every ounce of their presence, good or bad. Although Louisa left us scared, and caused many of our hearts to skip a beat, somehow we managed to close our eyes and sleep until morning's dawn made its appearance, and delivered us safely into the new day.

In the field beyond our curving driveway, in front of the old dilapidated barn that stood between our neighbors and us, is where we would ice skate on the rinks we made after the snow had fallen during the winter months. In the summer, this same field became our ballpark. Nine of us would play, dividing into two teams. I was often elected to pitch. The next player up after the one at bat, did the catching. Any balls hit within the baselines resulted in a hit. All balls hit into the outfield, were home runs. Anything hit beyond this point that crossed the paved road into the field across the street was the end of the game unless we could find the ball and then the game would resume.

At times, some of the older neighborhood boys would try to stake claim to our playing area, and Louisa would step in and help us shoo them away. No one messed with Louisa. She was a toughie.

Behind our house was the place I enjoyed spending much of my time during the summer months. There, not too far away from the road, was our swing set. I burned many daylight hours pumping my legs and letting the breeze blow through my hair and over my body, as I swayed back and forth. The harder I pumped my legs, the higher I would swing. At times, I was so high up in the air; it felt as if I could touch the sky. The movements were restful, and, even if just for a few moments, swinging afforded me an opportunity where I could be alone. I felt free to dream my dreams undisturbed. There would be no one else around me. It was just me, the swing and the sky. It felt SO good.

The barn, graying from years of service, held tools that lined the walls inside. Aging treasures stood on wooden shelves like statues. Sunlight filtered through the cracks in the wide boards that sheltered them. We were never allowed to enter the barn, yet, we were delighted to be able to peek through a rather large hole in one of the weather beaten slats. We could then get a glimpse of what was inside the darkened dusty barn. A little baby carriage stood out in front on the floor of the hayloft with an old trunk filled to the brim with other children's toys just a few steps away. As my eyes remained fixed on these items, my mouth began watering as I imagined myself owning such a beautiful carriage so I could push my doll around in the yard. It bothered me to know that the landlord had all of these potential toys collecting dust in the barn and yet never gifted them to us. Here we were four girls and 2 boys with just a few toys of our own, and there were all these unused toys among other treasures taking up space on the shelves. I never understood why the land-lord didn't offer these items to us, or even just allow us to borrow them?

Fallen boards on the right side of the barn, which piled up in a heap as they fell, became "forts." We made these forts with the boards and the flat head nails from the open wooden barrels that my father kept in the shed, along with the hammer and his other tools. Once the forts were made, we played imaginary "war games" with the wooden rifles the stocky women's husband, David, made for his sons at the lumber yard where he was currently employed, although, he was still working part time for the police department, too. The boys, all six of them, were the soldiers. Eventually one or two of them pretended to be wounded and needing first aid. A couple of us girls became the nurses that bandaged their wounds, and cared for them. We spent just as much time taking these forts down as our parents deemed them unsafe for us to keep up. Then, the boards would just be there in a pile with the other fallen boards along the side of the aging gray barn.

Large chestnut trees lined our road. Joining these were the apple trees that surrounded our house. The fall seasons brought many, many leaves. I can still remember the smell of freshly raked leaves, as we jumped into the piles we would make. My brothers had no fear and would jump right into these piles of leaves. I, however, tended to be a little more careful. I did not want to get hurt from any twigs or branches that may have been hiding amongst the leaves.

I never really understood what was so thrilling about jumping into a pile of leaves, and having to rake them all over again. The ritual of having to remove pieces of leaves or small sticks that got stuck in my hair was time consuming. If the leaves had any moisture on them, I would wonder if it was because of the night dew or from some other source my mind did not want to think about.

There were times when we would still be able to enjoy a bite or two from any of the worm-free apples that lingered behind after the frost. With the crushing movements of our jaws, the apples released their mouth-watering juices onto our tongues, and satisfied our taste buds. This would be a nice treat for us, as many times, we were still hungry after leaving the dinner table.

We weathered many trials that came our way over the years while we lived at the white house. Our food supply often went dry, and we never wore any of the trendy clothes in fashion during our school years. Mostly hand-me-downs covered our bodies, and left us knowing we were poor.

The long winter months were especially hard on us. It seemed there was never a short supply of white snow. After every snowfall, we would have to shovel the long driveway, so our father could drive the car close to the house when he returned home from work. There were times the snowdrifts were so high against the house barricading the doors that my brother Gabriel would have to climb out a window and rescue us from the snow that held us in our home like bait in a hunter's trap. Never, never, ever a dull moment at our house!

I used to love watching the fuel man dump coal down our chute until the bin below was full of plump hard rock coal. This would mean we would have heat! Because of the age of the house and the lack of insulation, it was not long before the last bits of coal tossed into the furnace left the coal bin empty again. Often, my parents would have to seek assistance from somewhere to secure that we would be warm and that we did not freeze.

It was here at the white house on the top of the hill, after I had turned ten in July that my mother gave birth to my sister, Mildred. It was November. Mildred was David's child. Everyone carried on as though Mildred was my father's child.

Many of our relatives chattered amongst themselves wondering if this was true. Was Gerard really Mildred's father? Mildred was without a doubt a spitting image of David. She had many of his facial features including the "glow" in her eyes when she smiled.

Emotional turmoil continued to show its ugly face around our home. At some point after Mildred was born, Irene determined that Edith was an unfit mother. Irene did not feel my mother had any "natural" love for her children. She did not feel my mother fed or clothed us properly. Irene tried to take us all away from my mother. I remember how scared I became after learning what Irene wanted to do, and panic built up inside me, causing my stomach to hurt. I wanted to run away (again). I began planning out an "escape" route in my mind, should Irene succeed in getting us. I was determined that this was not going to happen. I wasn't living with Irene!

While Louisa, Gabriel, Alan, Chloe', Aude, Mildred and I sat on the flowered slipcover that lay on the long couch that stood against the living room wall, my mother sat in a blue chair with Irene hovering over her like a lawyer defending a case in court. Irene questioned each one of us and aimed to know if we had any feelings for our mother. She wanted to see if she had our support and if we would be willing to come and live with her. Evidence on the faces of my siblings confirmed that I was not the only one that was afraid of the outcome of this night. It was clear that we were all afraid of Irene, my mother included. It was obvious that Gerard was a little nervous himself, as he never came out of his bedroom.

That night was probably the only time I can remember telling anyone that I loved my mother. Irene was furious to learn I was opting to stay with my mother. From this day forward, I knew I was going to have to endure many of Irene's evil schemes. My mother, for some reason, just sat there crying in the chair. Why didn't she tell this stocky woman to get out of her house and leave her family alone? She just sat there? What was this woman holding over my mother's head? What was my mother really doing that was so wrong? Better yet, what was "missing" that prevented her from defending herself and protecting her children? After I had children of my own, I knew that this was not normal. Instinctively, I would have been flying off my chair and lunging at Irene's throat if I had been in my mother's situation had Irene dared to even look at my child the wrong way. I know I would have even done much worse if she had hurt my child.

Fear enveloped my very body. It weighed on my soul to see my mother cry. My own hidden tears boiled inside me. I remember chanting silently in my mind that I hated Irene and my father. I hated everything they stood for. I silently prayed that they would run away again as they had when we lived at the slightly larger home and, if they didn't leave, I was hoping that somehow they would...DIE. If this was Irene's display of her love for us, I was all set. The only thing that might have made her house a little slightly more appealing than ours was the fact that somehow, even though she was in the same income bracket as us, there was always food in her cupboards.

When weighing the options of whether or not I would want to live with Irene, I knew that the little extra food was not going to compensate for the extra helping of abuse we would have received as she was even more abusive than our own mother already was. Edith was critical and negative, and always did something that would take away any joy we may have been able to reap around our situation, but Irene was wicked and enjoyed physically abusing us when she had the opportunity. Opportunities were plentiful. So, when it was my turn to give a reply, I made it clear I wanted to be with my mother.

The next day after church, we had to walk to Irene's house where my father would pick us up to bring us home. (We did this almost every Sunday). Irene accused me of lying the night before when I told her I loved my mother. In her anger, she kept hitting me. Many times I would have given in and told her what she wanted to hear, but there was more riding on this, and I was not going to be able to appease her that day. I didn't care how hard she hit me or how long she would keep hitting me, when she was done with her "routine," she was going to know that I still preferred my mother over her!

Like so many other times in our lives, my father sat in the background and did nothing. The same questions lingered. What was really going on that this former Marine and Police Officer would allow a woman to dominate and abuse his own wife and the children he fathered? Something was not right. There was more involved here than just a sexual relationship. My parents cowered to this woman. There had to be something she was holding over my parents.

How did Irene think that she would have been a more suitable guardian for us? Were the times she beat us with hairbrushes evidence of her love, and proof that she would be a better mother for us? Did Irene really feel she was a candidate for the "Mother of the Year" award? I think not!

After this, I was reluctant to trust anyone. In my eyes, Irene and my father were vicious—even more vicious than my peers who roamed the schoolyards and taunted me because I was different. (I wore a hearing aid). From here on out, my schoolteachers would take the brunt for the anger I had locked inside me. More importantly, no teacher was going to tell me what to do. I already had enough bosses at home, and I did not need any more. It did not matter that they wanted to teach me. I simply did not care. I would NOT listen to them!

School life as you would imagine was somewhat difficult. Chronic ear infections added greatly to my inability to hear. I had a hearing impairment. Most of my classmates were familiar with the reasons a person wore glasses. Many in the classroom wore them. None of these classmates knew anything about hearing aids or what it was like not being able to hear as they could. My deafness made me stand out as different. It kept me from hearing a large chunk of what was being said in the class whether I was in the front row or not as I was always told to demand on my first day of school. These were my mother's orders! I wanted to hide in a corner seat in the back row out of people's sight and out of people's minds! I would have preferred to disappear altogether! Running away wouldn't have changed this situation for me, as my deafness would come with me. I needed to learn to make the best of it, and move on.

I did not excel in the classroom. I found it difficult to understand many of the words being spoken around me. If I heard the question, I did not hear the answer. If I heard the answer, I did not know what the question had been. I could never put the two parts together. Although when I had time to read in between my all the "Cinderella" chores I had to do around the house, I loved how the pages of the book could transfer me into another world. A safer world and a world that was much, much further away.

I did enjoy reading a book now and then. However, my low self-esteem did not allow me to share my thoughts out loud. I would be terrified if my teacher asked me questions about the book I would be reading, and even though I could have answered any questions she might have had, I did not have the confidence to even try. When others made me feel I was stupid, I knew deep inside me that I was NOT stupid. Later on in life, I would explore several different avenues of interest just to prove this fact to myself. I simply did not hear like most people around me, and I couldn't understand why they couldn't see that my brain was perfectly intact.

Years later, I learned that I was a visual person. Faces, body movements and gestures were my primary language. It was not French. It was not English. I am thankful that my mother signed me up for special lip reading classes. Reading lips, along with any visuals, allowed me to understand most of the words I did not hear.

When I was eight years old, I received my first hearing aid. This should have been a blessing for me, but at times it caused me more frustrations. The general idea that most people have is that when you wear a hearing aid, you can hear normally. Well, yes and no. "Yes," you heard "all" the surrounding noises and the blah, blah, blah a little louder. But, "No," when it came to being able to hear and decipher the words I needed to hear. Louder sound does not always mean there is more defined word discrimination. It took years for me to understand this. So, I knew others did not have a clue either!

I spent many hours of my childhood observing my siblings as they went about their daily life when we were growing up. Each one of my siblings had a gift they could be proud of, even though they would never be encouraged to pursue their talents.

Louisa was smart and very sharp. She never rejected an opportunity to learn. She could be as caring as a mother hen should be as she watched over her chicks (us), and yet, she could be mean if we did not follow her rules when we were left in her care. Even though Louisa never read a "self-help" book on motherhood way back then, she knew that her siblings needed to be clean, fed and protected. It was kind of instinctive. She didn't have to be told what needed to be done, she just did it. What was preventing Edith, a grown woman from doing the same?

Gabriel liked the outdoors. He loved to follow the animal tracks that appeared in the winter's snow. He became good at being able to determine what kind of animals made the little prints in the snow. Eventually, he would use this keen sense to provide for himself later in life. He liked to cook although, under our circumstances, he probably did not like having to cook for his hungry siblings that awaited his nightly meals. He knew how to make hard caramel candy. He got the recipe from a science class he took. I loved this candy and the fact that he was willing to share some with me.

My brother Alan was funny. He was the class clown. He would and could do anything silly to make you laugh but not always at the best times. When being punished, his antics got us in deeper trouble. He was an extremely gifted artist. He had a distinct ability to draw athletes and make them come alive. You could see their movements in the way he drew his subjects.

Chloe' was my mother's favorite. She knew it, too. This did not take away the fact that she was my sister. She had a beautiful singing voice. In time, I did teach her how to play the guitar and, to this day, I believe it was my greatest gift to her. Later on, Chloe', Aude and I spent many hours playing guitar and singing together and entertaining for other people. This was the only thing we ever did together that made us feel united. Singing together made us look as if we were a family.

Aude was my favorite sister. She was caring and sweet. As a tomboy, she was fast. When she ran, her dirty blonde curls tightened as they lay in the glue of drops of sweat dripping on her forehead. She, too, could sing and enjoyed the positive attention music would bring her.

Mildred did not sing. Mildred did not talk much either. She was a private person who kept everything she thought inside her mind. She loved it when we read her stories when she was younger and, after learning to read herself, she continued to explore the excitements in any book she read. Books quenched a thirst within her that would never run dry. While her siblings played games around her, Mildred busied herself reading the pages of encyclopedias that were on the bookshelf. Other than for an occasional report we may have done for a school project, Mildred would be the only one that kept the dust off the covers of these books. She loved to learn about faraway places and often dreamed of visiting all these wonderful places she read about. Scotland, Ireland, Alaska were all like "homes" to her.

Lands she would someday visit if she had the opportunity to do so.

My father and my mother could both sing. They passed this trait and their love for music on to their children—Louisa, Gabriel and Alan included. The stocky woman and her husband did not sing. Finally, we had something in which they could not join in doing with us. Singing was something we did not have to share with them.

Many times when I would play guitar and sing songs, or when Chloe', Aude and I would have our practice sessions, I came to realize that these moments were the only times I noticed that Irene had any peace. It would be the only time I can remember when she did not cause us any trouble. She just sat back and listened. It is amazing the effect that simple music can have over one's aura.

The instinct to survive is in the DNA of all humans. Whether we know it or not, it is there. It motivates us to keep getting up and trying when we are unable to or when we no longer physically want to. This becomes a protective drive for us: a subconscious guide that allows us to keep fighting and to keep on enduring.

I feel that within the hearts and souls of each of my siblings that we all had the desire to seek out better lives than the lives we experienced during our earlier years. What our parents had done to themselves and allowed to happen to us shattered many of our dreams. We would never become the people we were supposed to be. Still, what we endured made us stronger to some degree. We were determined that when we ventured out on our own, we were going to make serious changes and make better choices. This would be a good thing.

# CHAPTER FIVE

## The White House on Top of the Hill (Part Two)

O ur older home had a unique feature I had never seen before. The stairs leading to the second floor of our home were steep. But, just before you got to the top of the stairs, on the left, was a small room. This room was used over time to store household furnishings and unwanted items. Many of these items were still in good condition. Their previous owners could not throw them away and they left these items behind when they moved away. Just think about it for a minute. "Hidden treasures" were in a "hidden room" in my home where there were "hidden secrets." Hmm… The good thing is that I did not see any "locks" on the door. I knew if I ventured in every now and then to look around, I was feeling safe knowing I would be able to escape should any other "hidden" unknown and mysterious "anything" be in the room with me.

Amongst the "unwanted" items was some fancy dishware. I loved the green depression glassware that shined after removing the dust. These stood pretty on the dining room shelves that held them. There were also some rose colored glassware just waiting for someone—anyone—to pick them up. So, I did and I loved holding these when no one was around to yell at me for playing with them. I imagined what it was like to have used these precious gems that had been preserved from years gone by.

Heating this house was like throwing money out the window. There were many drafts and open spaces for the warm heat to escape. These cold spots sucked out the warmth that should have been warming our bodies as we went about our daily lives. To supplement for the lack of coal in the coal bin, Gabriel would wander about the property and collect any fallen limbs, sticks or wood that laid about to be used to help keep us warm. His young body would chop any pieces too large to fit into the rusting furnace that would burn them. This was a huge responsibility for a young lad not to mention an embarrassing one since his friends all lived in modern houses equipped with base board heating. Still, Gabriel deserves many thanks for his efforts in helping us to keep warm.

Outside my father's bedroom was a door leading to the scary, dark, eerie and spider ridden cellar. The wooden stairs were falling apart from all the years of use. Once, as I was going down the stairs, I lost my footing and, after tumbling down the remaining stairs, I landed in this giant-sized spider web against the wall by the bottom step. The web was thick and had this gooey looking stuff in it. I was not sure if it was just some gooey moisture or if they were some icky "eyes" peering out at me. Even if I had broken all my bones when I fell, the fright I was feeling at this time would have motivated me to stand up QUICKLY AND RUN! As I tried to recoup from my fall, I could see there were spiders on me and I could not move fast enough to brush these off me. All I could think of were some of the scenes from movies I had seen at the theaters, and I was imagining that these spiders would spin their webs around me and I would not be able to escape. As depicted in the movies, I would later be killed when they ATE me or when I died from FRIGHT! Either way, I was not hanging around to find out!

I am still traumatized by this memory and if this wasn't enough, the creepy hatchway that stood on the left side of the cellar had stairs leading out their doors and always seemed to hold chips of wood or pieces of chewed "something" that was left behind by a furry creature that may have passed by. I didn't like going into the basement as it seemed that spiders were common renters in the dusty, musty little corners. It also seemed that, when it rained, the stairs would absorb some of the wetness, which left the basement damp and smelling disgusting. The cellar generated an eerie feeling inside me every time I had to go down to stoke the furnace or add another shovel of coal to the existing fire.

The coal bin in the basement was across from the furnace. A small window above the coal bin is where the fuel man inserted a metal chute that let the pieces of coal fill the wooden bin that held them. To the left of the coal bin, a heavily worn board hung on the wall. It still held a bridle for a horse that must have belonged to those who had lived here at one time. The leather was old, and it appeared that it would just fall apart if we were to ever touch it. Nevertheless, I tried to imagine the history that may have surrounded the evidence on this one piece of wood that was still hanging in our dirt cellar. Believe me when I say I had quite an imagination!

Behind the furnace was an opening that allowed one to crawl out of the house when in danger or when under attack years ago by Indians. I thought about the worries and the fears that may have come over the people who lived in the house then, and I would quickly close the furnace door and climb the stairs as fast as I could until I was safely behind the door at the top of the stairs. I did not like this basement, and I would have to fight off the images that my mind procured about what may have happened to the people who lived in this house during these times, and the hardships that may have weighed them down.

Winters were cold. Despite how I felt about winter, it came around every year no matter how hard I prayed. Winter also brought with it the holiday seasons. It meant the schools we attended would close for the day. Sometimes the schools would close for a couple of weeks. I didn't look forward to vacations. Yet along with my siblings, we did try and find fun things to occupy ourselves from time to time.

Playing inside the home was reserved for rainy days and blizzards only. When the sun came up and after eating our breakfast, we washed the dishes and put them away in the cupboards. We would then dress in the warmest clothing we owned, and our mother would usher us outside to play until lunchtime.

The fallen chicken coop a little distance away from the hatchway leading to the cellar became our playground after a snowstorm. Inches of clean, fresh, fallen snow piled up on the hill and covered most of the fallen boards that froze near what remained of a former chicken coop. The coop was about halfway down the hill. Gabriel made a path for us, and we were able to slide down this hill with our cardboard or plastic sleds—or with the newer metal saucers that Irene and David's children would bring with them when they visited. At night, Gabriel watered down the path and made it icy for us the next day.

Starting from the top of the hill, we would hop on our sleds and begin our decent. The speed would take us sailing on the new path made over the heap of fallen boards and sent us flying into the air until the air held us no more. Then, we would fall. We would land on any leftover foliage still showing above the snow. These bushes cushioned our fall as we came in for landing. There were times we were not so lucky and flew a little further out. Then, we would then land in a patch of thorny brush instead. Ouch!

We patiently waited to take our turns. Hours passed as we continued to slide and fly. Over the course of the winter months, we repeated this sledding ritual. We enjoyed every moment we spent on this icy hill and the path that we made over the coop. The warmth in our hearts took away any coldness we should have felt. The thrill we got from the rides on this icy hill outweighed any other rides we would take at amusement parks we visited in our lifetime. It was the most fun we ever enjoyed together as children.

Not everyone shared our joy, however. Once when returning home from the night shift of his new job, our father saw us having fun and, for a little while, he stood at the top of the hill watching us as we each took our turns sliding down the icy hill. We begged him to "just try it once." Eventually, we were able to coerce him into taking this magical ride and flying through the air.

Despite the few flickers of fun we enjoyed when playing together outside, it took just a few moments after coming back inside the home for the reality of our "real life" to quickly resurface. Fun times could not take away the burden we experienced because of our poverty. We were poor. We knew that we were poor. Our classmates, neighbors and town folks all knew we were poor. Many times we went to school without a proper lunch or the funds to purchase a hot meal. Often, I would migrate to the end of the lunch line so that my classmates would be seated and eating their lunches unlikely to notice when I had to sign my name on an "IOU" meal ticket. Adding to this, we rarely wore new clothes or had new shoes to wear to school. Hand-me-downs were a given. Still, we did welcome these items, and we were not too proud to wear them.

Many times, Edith would send us to bed without our supper. It was her way of punishing us for something we might have done that displeased her. When I look back and think about this, I wonder if the real reason she sent us to bed was to hide the fact that there was not enough food to go around. If we were sent to bed, there would be more food to feed the younger siblings. The more I thought about these times, it was now all starting to make a lot of sense to me. I mean really. How bad could we have been? After a while, even a child learns to do whatever he needed to do to stay out of trouble so he could get his needs met.

Feelings of hunger troubled me throughout my child-hood. When I was old enough to earn my own money, I found comfort in the food I could then buy for myself. When living on my own, I needed to have a full cupboard of food and meat in the freezer at all times. I still have this need even today. When the cupboards get low in supplies, it creates a kind of depression within me that I cannot seem to get around. This depression will linger until the cupboards once again hold an abundance of food items.

Despite being poor, there was a time when most of my siblings each had a bicycle of their own. Regularly during the summer vacations from school, we would all ride down to a farm just over the state line a few miles away from our house. The farmer would let David and my father go on his property and shoot their guns in the thick of the trees.

On special occasions, my mother and David took us to the farm where we would pitch our tents and camp out. While the children collected firewood, David and my mother got the campfire started. We then sat around the warm fire and roasted marshmallows. We would eat any other treat my mother packed to ward off any chance of our being hungry until breakfast in the morning. I appreciated the smoke from the fire as it gave relief from the flies, nasty mosquitoes and other insects that came around and feasted on my blood.

Once, I found myself alone on this farm with David. I do not remember why I would happen to be there alone with him and not with any of my other siblings. Perhaps I had been lagging behind when the others had already started on their journey back home. I had been trying to catch the barn kittens as they peeked in and out of the cracks in the wooden slats near the barn by the fence that kept the cows in the pasture.

David wanted to show me something in the barn and wanted me to go inside the barn with him. In the middle of the floor was an old antique car. He motioned for me to come closer to him so he could show me a specific detail on the car. As I came closer, he grabbed me and was trying to molest me. I struggled with him and was able to break free from his hold. I ran out of the barn as fast as my legs could run, got on my bike and began pedaling as fast as I could towards home.

David caught up with me, and we rested at the top of the long steep hill that made us too tired to pedal anymore. He proceeded to sit down next to me on the grass by the gate of the cemetery, and grossly started to masturbate in front of me. His tongue hung out the side of his mouth. As he chewed on his tongue, I remembered thinking how "crazy" he looked. His behavior was scaring me and fear began to overtake me. I was not sure what he was doing to himself, but it did not look normal in any way, shape or form.

I was about ten years old. I got up from the ground and ventured into the cemetery. I had to get away from him. In my panic, I did not have a chance to imagine what harm could have come to me from amongst the gravestones of the old cemetery as depicted in some of the horror movies I had seen. I hated those movies. I would not care if I never saw another movie for the rest of my life. At this time, though, I had my own "horror flicks" going on inside my head, and the scenes I was imagining had me scared!

When David was finished doing his "business," he smiled his filthy grin at me and we left. This would not be the last time I would see him enjoying the pleasure of his own body, or having to ward off his attempts when trying to enjoy mine. There was something to be said about this grin. It had GUILT written all over it! If David was flashing this smile after not attempting something with me, then, for sure, this guilt would be the result of his trying to gain sexual pleasures with someone else or something else. My own "secrets" were starting to accumulate in my mind and it was becoming unbearable for me to keep them shut up inside. I often, wanted to SCREAM, but for whatever reason or reasons, I kept silent.

Many years later, I shared the memories of these bitter times with my sister Louisa and she confided to me that David had done similar things around her. She, too, was fully aware of David's "grin." Thirty years would pass before I dared to release the bars that held these "secret" memories in the prison of my mind.

Weekends were hard to endure. It seemed that David and my mother would leave our house after we had our supper. I never knew where they were going or when they were coming back. My father and Irene were in charge when they were gone. Right from the start, it seemed to me that Irene enjoyed hurting others and would always manage to be mad at one of us so she could administer physical discipline. She would hit us or beat us until she got the response she wanted from us.

If we denied doing something she accused us of doing, she would smack us around until we admitted our fault. There were times my father would force admission by using his belt even though we had not disobeyed. Many times, I had to witness events like these as my siblings were beaten or subjected to degrading evils from the hands of this woman and my father.

After admitting to my "crime," Irene would make me sit in a corner in the dining room for hours as the other kids watched television in the living room, the next room over. At some point, usually a couple of hours later, Irene would come and talk with me. She would tell me, she would "never have to punish me if I would just tell her the truth." Then, she would tell me how much she "loved me" and would wait for me to say that I loved her too. Thereafter, she would give me a cookie or a piece of candy and let me leave the corner so I could go to bed. I longed for the comfort of my bed and the security that I felt when I was tucked under the blankets. The ordeal would be over for me, at least, for today.

I still cringe inside as I recall the memories that filled my mind from the abuses we endured while living at the white house on the top of the hill. Some tactics used by Irene and my father were so horrifying that I cannot bring myself to put them in writing. I pray that these incidences that have escaped the memories of some of my siblings never return to their minds. Nothing would be the same for them should they remember what they had had to endure.

A lifetime of decades had past and whenever I hash over these days gone by with some of my siblings today, I can sense their anger and their pain is still very much alive. I see the scars they carry with them because of these events. The wounds we received from the lives we lived at the hands of these four adults still linger as a result of the physical, sexual abuses and the neglect. Time has not been sufficient to heal these wounds. These continued to fester.

Mainly, many of my siblings harbored a deep resentment over the lack of loving care our individual parents failed to provide over all the other hardships we had to endure. They had made us victims of the games they played. Symptoms of mental illnesses have cropped up in many of my siblings, and I, Julianne, was not spared the consequences resulting from nightmares and deep depression. I so longed for a time when each one of us will be freed from the pains, which are still holding us captive to various degrees today.

If the hardships, embarrassments and individual pains we were currently facing were not enough, my heart started pounding irregularly again when I started hearing my parents having discussions about our having to move again. They were not just talking about moving to another house in the area, but they were talking about relocating to the BIG city! What?? Oh, dear!

# CHAPTER SIX
## The Green House

We did move just as I had been hearing my parents talk about. This time when we moved, my parents found us a home to rent in Springfield, Massachusetts. The white house on the top of the hill needed extensive repairs especially to the heating system. As usual, my parents were behind in their rent, and the owners were not interested in taking money from their own pocketbook to make the needed changes. Our coal furnace had not passed the fire code when the insurance company came around to inspect our home for their records. One week before the start of the new school year, we were moving our belongings into our new living quarters. I had just turned fourteen years old.

The new house would be the largest of all the houses we had lived in. Fading green tiles covered the outside of the three-story house. The nicest feature was the large porch in the front of the house. We spent many summers sitting on this porch, talking or just watching the daily activities going on around us in the neighborhood.

Our new home had thirteen rooms. Plenty of room to

care for the needs of our immediate family, and for the space needed when eleven children and four adults shared this same space on weekends. To my surprise, I had my own bedroom on the third floor—my own bedroom. This meant that I had this room all to myself. Yeah!

My mother Edith's bedroom was on the first floor. I loved the French doors that would swing open when you entered her room. My parents often retreated to this room when they had private conversations they did not want the children to hear. On the weekends my mother shared her room; not with my father, but with David.

We had a large kitchen on the first floor. Every night during the week except for a few here and there, my mother and David would enjoy their tea and toast with jam as they sat eating these at our yellow table. Occasionally, my mother had cottage cheese with a drizzle of frozen strawberries on top. Every weekday, David came to our home after having had his supper with his own "family." He would then spend his evening hours at our house "drooling" over my mother as he kept his eyes focused on her while they conversed. It was evident that he worshipped the ground she walked on and was entertained by her words. They carried on every night all the while my father was sleeping in his bedroom, which by the way, was on the second floor directly above where they were sitting.

The living room had many windows. In fact, there were many windows in this house. I did not like washing them in the spring when we did "spring cleaning." But more importantly, I especially wanted to keep the win-dows in the living room dirty so that people could not see inside our house. Why did I feel this way? Well, just a few short weeks after we had moved, Edith had decided to spruce up the living room with lively colors and painted the fireplace a bright gaudy orange color. I was told that my mother chose this paint scheme because the colors made the mantel and the large mirror above the mantel stand out more.

Still, even worse than this, was the fact that the chair and sofa no longer displayed the maple wood that used to surround the soft cushions. Their arms and frames were now painted a dark olive green color. These must have been the trendy colors of the early 1960's. I truly wished that I could have gone to the store to buy "blackout" curtains to hide this "makeover." Martha Stewart would NOT have approved! I had never seen anything like this.

I remember the first time I saw the color scheme. After I got over the shock of seeing the drastic color changes, I was embarrassed to know we owned this horrid looking furniture. I was never going to invite any of my friends (if I made any at the new school, of course) over to my house. I did not want the whole school finding out about the orange fireplace and the green-painted furniture, and give them something else to tease me about. I was sure they were already going to tease me about the fact that I wore a hearing aid. (They did!) I don't really know why wearing this amplification device seemed so horrible to me except the fact that NO ONE ELSE at school wore one. Once again, I was going to stand out amongst my peers. This would be on top of the shame and disgrace I was already carrying on my young shoulders because of my parents' involvement with Irene and David.

The dining room was big. The extra space allowed ample room to hold the many meals we would share with others at times, but mostly with the stocky woman, her husband and their children when they feasted at our home on the weekends and during holidays.

It was thirteen stairs to the second floor where my father, Gerard, had his bedroom. He had a dresser, a double bed, and a little end table in his room. It was here on this little table that Irene would place her glass bottle of golden yellow Prince Matchabelli when she slept with my father on the weekends. Golden fiber curtains hung over the two windows that filtered light into the mostly darkened room. Gerard was still driving a truck, and was currently working the night shift. He slept during the day and, for this reason, he kept his room void of much sunlight.

Although he spent most of his time in his room sleeping, there was another secret held within its walls. Sorrow and deep depression kept my father a prisoner in his room. The "warden" was the various bottles of alcohol he drank, and hid beneath the top mattress. Once the bottles were surrounded by the metal coil springs, the coils protected the bottles and kept them from breaking. My father, among other things, was an alcoholic. It was clear to me that he drank and tried to hide from the problems that were troubling him. However, they did not go away. I do not remember ever seeing my father truly happy. He was hurting deep within himself. Somehow, I could feel his pain and it troubled me to some degree as I could not change any of it for him. I could not put a Band-Aid on his hurting soul and make it better.

Remnants of a second kitchen was down the hall from my father's bedroom. We referred to this room as our "playroom, art room or junk room." It had a large white kitchen table with chairs where the children would play cards or some of the board games we owned on the weekends. During the week, we did our homework, if we had any, or we played our music in this room. It was also in this room that our dog "Buddy," who we later discovered was a girl and renamed "Buddy Girl," mothered her many puppies.

The junior high school where I would complete 8th and 9th grades was literally fifty steps outside the front door of my home. I could see the desk where I would sit in my homeroom when I looked out my third floor bedroom window.

When reflecting back on these school years, I can still taste the bitterness my actions left behind. Every day, I would enter school LATE! Now mind you, I didn't have to walk to a bus stop or to the end of a driveway to catch a bus. Just a hop, skip, and a jump—and boom, I should have been sitting at my desk. No, not me. It never happened. Each morning, I had to walk my sister, Mildred, to the babysitter before I went to school. It did not matter to me how cute Mildred was dressed or how I brushed her hair. The fact was that Mildred did not walk fast and certainly could not keep up with me. Even though she was smart, she walked very, very slow. Trying to hurry Mildred was useless. On our way to the babysitter, we would pass my schoolmates walking in the opposite direction and all the while Mildred dragged her six foot, knitted monkey behind her. It took me forever to get her to where she needed to be. Frustrated, humiliated and late, I was always rushing to get to school.

Understandably, I was not a happy camper. The facts were clear as to why I was not happy. One, I had to get Mildred to her sitter, rain or shine and, of course, snow! Two, I could have walked the same distance twenty times to the one Mildred walked in the same amount of time it would have taken me to do the twenty. Thirdly, I knew my classmates were always wondering why I was not going to school but instead was seen walking in the wrong direction according to the needle on their compass. Reason number four was having to be seen with someone who dragged a gigantic, life-sized stuffed monkey by its long tail as they walked. Reason number five was the fact that I knew my peers were aware that I lived only a few inches from the school so they could not understand why I was late—AGAIN. And lastly, reason number six, was having to continue this routine for each day my school was in session, and this was taxing on my nerves.

Mr. Zippin, my homeroom teacher, got the brunt of my anger. Every day, I tested his stamina and pushed his buttons to see how far I could go. His "suit of armor" sported many dents. Still, my daggers of rudeness and vulgarity were not enough to penetrate the steel of his armor. When I left his classroom, Mr. Zippin could still be seen standing in front of the room bravely awaiting his next group of students.

Today, I am truly sorry for my attitude and the lack of respect I failed to give my teachers. I often wished I could turn back the clocks and let them know this, especially Mr. Zippin. I had a lot of anger building up inside me. Just as a lit firecracker eventually will explode, unfortunately, I let some of this mounting pressure inside me out at school. I did not wait to let a little out here and there during the course of the day. No, I started as soon as I entered the classroom!

I did not make it easy for these teachers to teach me. So much was going on in the home now, that quite frankly, I did not care about school or myself to warrant any changes in my behavior. At this time in my life, I did not have a single ounce of scholastic ambition. I wish I had been able to explain to someone why I was feeling this way. I so much wanted to expose the truths about the abuses, the affair and the lies going on in my home just a few feet from the school itself. But I couldn't just yet. I kept silent as now was not the right time to let others know the truth. (Was there really ever going to be a right time?)

Even though relatives and just about everyone we met questioned the possibility of an affair or reasons for our continued involvement with Irene and her family, no one ever really came forward to offer us aid or to help stop it. Relatives voiced their strong opinions and feelings around the issue of the mystery hidden behind our closed doors, but they never did anything about it. They just simply stayed away. When it came to putting their money where their mouths were, they did not have a penny of courage to step forward and confront Edith and Gerard.

For years, I always thought that my mother was a victim of circumstances. Circumstances I thought she could not escape. However, in looking back now, I started remembering much more than my memory wished to expose. Edith should have acted to protect her children. She should have sought protection for herself. She knew that Irene was abusive to her children. Why did she allow her children to be abused? It seemed to me that eventually the truths about the wife-swapping escapades and her part in them and the traumas her children had to endure should have, at some point, in her life come back to haunt her. These same questions should be directed to Gerard, too. If he truly loved my mother, he should have taken action and got on his white horse, scooped Edith up onto the saddle, and galloped away with her. It was evident to me at my young age that Gerard loved my mother. Irene would just be a shoo-in for getting what he was missing, and what he was not receiving in the bedroom. He wanted a warm body by his side. He wanted to be held. And, he wanted his physical needs met. Irene was a willing prospect, and she was better than having nothing at all.

It is hard for me to believe the choices Edith made as a mother and as a woman. If she was not happy being married to my father and "so in love" with David, I don't understand why she did not just divorce my father. If she did love my father, why didn't she do something to gain back the control she had of him before the wife-swapping started?

I understand as a Catholic that there were restrictions on issues of divorce. Church traditions did not allow its communicants to divorce and remarry at this time in history. Yet, I wonder if she ever meditated on the price she was going to have to pay for her years of adultery, lies, stealing and coveting. The long road ahead led to many wrong turns in my mother's life, and it was evident by the consequences she was reaping. My mother, however, was not the only one who did not make good choices. My father was also struggling to align a moral compass.

It became apparent that there were other men who involved themselves in our lives every now and then, and they were not always interested in my mother. These men considered themselves to be in positions of great importance. More "luggage" presented itself within the folds of my memory. My brain did not want to remember anymore. I could not stop these unpleasant thoughts from escaping out of their hiding places. These new found memories were now setting off a new batch of questions that, at present, would remain unanswered. Ugh! I hate mysteries! Many times, I would pray for some kind of normalcy. With everything I had witnessed so far in my life, I don't even think I would have been able to identify with anything that WAS normal.

The horrors of having to deal with the issues around the different abuses from the four adults for the past nine years was not going to be easy for any of us to shed. When my father was drinking, all of the children living at home walked on egg shells. When my mother was frustrated, you had to make sure you didn't upset her and send her off on one of her two hour screaming fits. When Irene was around, you were always wondering when her moods would change or when she would start picking on us, mainly me. When David was in the house, you did not want to be alone with him. Our list of woes we had endured just kept getting longer and longer. What next? I really did not want the answer to this question as I was positive in due time the answers would be revealed to me.

Somehow, despite all the money my father and mother made from working, we were always in a financial crisis. I don't know where the money went, but most times we were late on our rent, did not have adequate food or clothing and we never went anywhere. We never went on a vacation or frequented any fancy restaurants in the area. Where did their money go? Another mystery that remains unsolved even to this day.

To help meet the family's financial needs (or for some other reason I do not know about), Gerard began to run numbers for a local crime organization. On top of his drinking problem, he might have been a gambler. I imagine this newest situation on top of the consequences of his already sick lifestyle may have been reason enough for my father to want to drink even more.

There were times Gerard spent the "winnings" that belonged to others and he found himself in deep trouble—big time. He put his life in grave danger many times when he did this. How could he not care about the harm that could have come his way? Or the harm he could have brought upon his family? What was he thinking?

Several times while we were living in the green house, strange men took time out from their "booking" schedules to pay my father a visit. On one particular visit, these "men" told my father that if he did not pay up FAST, they were going to break his legs. Their first warning!

Then, the "soft talking" began in my mother's bedroom. Phone calls to Irene and David were made. My father's face would be very pale when he left my mother's bedroom. My mother was scared. Even though she did not say so with words, evidence of fear was apparent in her eyes.

Louisa remembers this night as Irene had approached her to see if she had any money set aside that she could "borrow." Even Irene was scared. My father needed money FAST! Taking money from these "men" was not a good thing.

Shortly after having received his first warning, a dark Cadillac pulled up in front of our house. My brother Alan was bouncing a ball off the side of our house when the window in the back of the car was being lowered revealing a man trying to get my brother's attention. The man with a funny looking nose in the back seat leaned forward to question Alan. He wanted to know if my father was at home. After Alan had nodded that he was not, the man told my brother that it was very "important that my father get in touch with him and very soon." No names, no phone numbers were needed. The man said my father knew who he was. Then, the Cadillac drove off.

I had been observing this scene from the front porch. I did not know who these men were. Even though I figured that their presence must have had something to do with money, I knew these were not your typical "bill collectors." On top of the trials we faced on a regular basis, we were now adding terror to the list of things we had to deal with. Men wearing dark glasses were showing up at our home in their large dark cars and wanted to hurt my father. Why would they want him to wear "cement shoes?" Why did these men want to hurt my father? Fear I had been feeling on the inside of my home was added to the fear I was now facing on the outside of the home.

As you can imagine, daily living became confusing and was engrained with many different trials. By this time, Louisa had already left the confines of my parents' care. While living in the white house, sickness and stresses caused by the "secrets" of what was going on within the walls of our home created serious medical problems for Louisa. Her illness went neglected. When my mother "finally" took her to get professional medical attention, her condition had gotten critical. I remember conversations around the fact that Louisa may have to have her leg or legs amputated. I did not like what I was hearing and I was very afraid for Louisa.

Irene jumped into action in Louisa's behalf, and sought out a second medical opinion. After the doctor examined the situation, he told Irene that he did not care where Louisa went when she left his office but she was NOT to return to her home! The doctor was appalled by my sister's condition. Blue lines were appearing on her body and these were evident that there was blood poisoning. She would need "proper" care to heal. She needed a "safe haven" as they call them today. She needed to get away from the everyday stresses going on in her life.

After leaving the doctor's office, Louisa went to live with Irene and David and their children. This was supposed to be a temporary arrangement. Irene promised Louisa that she would take good care of her and would give her all the love she wanted. Louisa was craving love and she needed to get her health back so arrangements were made for her to move in with Irene and David.

In time, Louisa's body healed. But, all was not well with Louisa. Events that transpired while living with Irene and David would become another disastrous chapter in her life as time would later reveal. I did not want Louisa to leave us. Being a child, I did not have the final say in this matter. In fact, I didn't have any say. I could sense in my heart that this move was not going to be good for Louisa. I don't know how she thought Irene could offer her any sort of healthy love, but children are hopeful, and I am sure she was hoping for a reprieve from the current home life she was living. Boy was she fancy-fooled!

I hated the fact that Louisa was living away from us. I wanted her to come home, where she belonged. I missed her. This brought to my mind something else I did not understand. Relatives claimed they did not like this arrangement when they heard about it, but none of them came forward to assist. Again, they did a lot of chattering amongst themselves, and again, not one of them came forward or took any action to help us in this situation. Why didn't they? Why did they stand back and let bad things happen to Louisa? How could they just close their eyes? They knew something was not right in our home. I will never understand this.

School staff wondered why I did not know when Louisa was marked absent when she wasn't at school. They would ask me to explain her absence after I had been called to the office. I told them the truth when they questioned me. Louisa was staying at Irene and David's home. The school made a phone call to our house, and this brought serious trouble my way when I returned home from school later that afternoon. Basically, most of the yelling around this event was to pound into my brain that "I was not to disclose what went on inside our home to anyone!"

After Louisa did get well, she did not come home as planned. I could not for the life of me figure out why my parents did not go and get her. How could they just turn their backs on her and let her walk away? It tore me apart inside. My questions and the pain I was feeling were not to be shared. I kept them inside my soul. Telling the police, the relatives or others would have caused me more problems. They probably would not have believed me anyway. It would only give others more gossip to spread around about our already disgusting family.

Faced with situations like these almost every day of my life did not make going to school easy. I did not do well in school. I simply could not manage another thing on my plate. With Louisa gone, I became the new caretaker of the younger siblings while my parents were at work. Gabriel had a job after school. So being the next oldest child in the family, I was now carrying the load previously handled by Louisa and Gabriel. Schoolwork was just too heavy of a burden for me to carry. I did not have energy to do homework. Of course, this got me in greater trouble with the teachers, and added to my woes. Detention was given but I did not care. I just prayed that I would be home from school in time to make supper and have the house clean before Edith got home from work. Edith was loud and when she was angry, everyone in the neighborhood heard her words.

I was sinking into a very deep depression. I did not have the liberty of being able to imagine myself out of this mess. Pain left behind as a result of the physical abuse, the anguish of having to observe when my siblings were abused, the constant put-downs and criticisms, having to continue fighting to keep others from sexually abusing me, the embarrassment of living in a home centered around the four-way affair, enduring the consistent state of fear, my father's alcoholism, and now the situation with Louisa. I truly had a full plate. When I look back on these years and remember my own unhealthy thoughts I had invading my mind, it ceases to amaze me that not only had I survived these years, but I had not given up! I am positive someone was watching over me.

School became a place to hide. I did not want to be called on. I did not want to participate in the classroom. I did not want anyone to speak to me. I just needed time away from our house. This would not be good for Mr. Zippin. He did not need me starting his morning off with a bunch of grief and antics that could eventually cause him to have ulcers. I gave him a hard time about rules he set or about what he wanted me to do especially regarding the rules he had on chewing gum in the classroom. It did not matter how many times Mr. Zippin would tell me to throw my gum away. I had it covered! I took a good supply of gum with me each time I went to school. In fact, I went to the corner drug store and bought five packs of gum every morning before going to school. So, "NO," cooperation was not in my vocabulary. If he had a thermos in his desk, I can bet he would have wanted it to contain more than just coffee. He probably could have used something a little stronger.

I wanted to let Mr. Zippin know why I was angry. I knew he would want to help me if he knew as he did care about his students. Therefore, I had to make him dislike me or, at least, my behavior so that he would keep his distance and not involve himself in my behalf. I still did not trust anyone at this time. During these school years, anger continued to build its walls around me. I had to keep silent. I, yes I, Julianne, was very smart and always managed to find ways to rebel and let out some steam. Not always in a healthy way, but what did I know?

When I was sixteen, my parents bought me my first guitar. There were no lessons or books of instructions. They only gave me a guitar and the case. At first, I tinkered with it trying to make sense of the strings and the many different sounds they made. Then, I would put it away. When I did not pick up the guitar and strum it every now and then, Edith would scold me for not trying to learn how to play it. In the beginning, the guitar placed another burden on my shoulders.

One day, I saw David with my guitar on his lap. When he looked up at me, he flashed his "grin" and gave me the "what are you going to do about it" look? I was very angry. He had touched my guitar without asking me permission first. I also wondered what he had been doing in my bedroom in the first place. From this day forward, I vowed that I would play the guitar at every possible moment I had free or when David was at our home. I did this just to keep David from being able to touch it.

In time, I did learn a few chords and I did figure out how to use them to play songs. I would sing along as I strummed the chords. I found refuge in my songs and singing gave me a chance to release some of the tensions

I held within my soul. As I had not wanted David to touch any part of my body, I also did not want his "hands" touching anything I owned, which included my guitar!

At some point, my sister Chloe' became interested in learning to play the guitar and I taught her as much as I knew. She then would join me when I played. As we sang, we would harmonize together. This gave us each some much needed boosts of self-esteem. Eventually, my sister Aude also became interested in joining us and her voice added to the beauty of the songs we sang.

The years were quickly passing by. The children of both families were growing older. Even though I did graduate from high school, I did not go to my graduation. Edith had made it clear to me that she would NOT attend my graduation ceremony. Considering my past school history, she felt that my presence and hers would be hypocritical. This was true. I mean what had I really accomplished? I took up "space" in the classroom—period! My diploma came to me in the mail.

Shortly after graduation, I had gotten my license and my very first car. Having my own transportation brought with it some bonuses: mainly liberty! Gerard had taken me to a car dealership to help me look at cars I might want to purchase. Unfortunately, like most other times in my life, my father was drunk and his presence was more of an embarrassment then helpful. I regretted having to be with him in public when he drank. I personally did not know anything about cars, but I did purchase a car that day: a sporty Ford Galaxy 500, white with red interior and a convertible. I was thrilled to be having my own set of wheels.

In some ways, the car allowed me the freedom to do what I wanted to do and go places I wanted to go. It was also helpful in getting my three younger sisters and me out of the house and away from the grips of the adults. We did not have favorable conditions in the home, and being able to leave for a couple hours here and there was helpful.

Staying home meant someone was not going to have a good day. Was Edith having one of her fits? Was Gerard drunk again? Was Irene looking for someone to beat on? Was David wishing he could gain sexual pleasures from someone? You never did know what awaited you at home. It was best to stay out as long as you could. It was much safer this way.

The abuses from the four adults continued to add height to the angry walls around me. I wanted things to be different: loving and calmer. As much as I willed to change my feelings, the walls just got higher and higher. Most of my anger was pointed at my father. He provided for us financially, but he never protected us. When I looked at my father, I saw nothing more than a coward.

As I mentioned earlier, there were many other "men" involved in my mother's life. I had come downstairs as my father was just getting off the phone with someone. As I lingered about in the kitchen, I could hear some of the conversations that my parents were having. It was very serious. I was not able to hear any real specifics around this situation except the fact that one of my mother's male workmates had committed suicide. Rumor had it this man was a gambler and had big money problems. I, however, beg to differ on this issue. I mean, why was he calling our house? And what did my father have to do with this? Did he owe my father money? Or, was he involved somehow with my mother? Any of these situations may have left this "mysterious man" feeling like he was going to be hurt badly by my father.

As anyone could imagine, I had trouble falling asleep that night. I could tell by the look on my mother's face that she was in trouble. Many questions were now beginning to form in my head. What had she done? And, who was going to be mad at her? This time, Gerard did not look mad at her, but he was scared for her. I could only toss and turn in my bed. Sleep would not come. I would lay there and wonder when this trouble would begin.

Most of the answers to my questions were answered later the next day. Getting caught cheating on David was not a good thing. I can remember hearing David screaming at my mother behind the closed French doors to her bedroom. When I heard my mother crying on the other side of these doors, I attempted to open the doors to see what was going on. My father who was standing at the edge of the living room across the hall from the bedroom stopped me from going into the bedroom and told me to "let it alone." He waved his arms and motioned for me to leave.

In the past, I had been a victim of many of David's screaming rages. So now, even though I could not see through the closed doors, I did not need to open them to know what was happening. I already knew. David would be in my mother's face, spitting as he screamed, maybe even chewing on his tongue. Evidence of fear would surely be on my mother's face and in her eyes. It would not matter how many tears my mother cried. These would not be enough to tame David's anger. My mother would have to endure the torment until he grew tired of screaming or until he screamed the anger out of his system.

In time, my mother emerged from her bedroom with red eyes and tear stains on her cheeks. There were bruises and redness around her neck. David's grip had been so tight around her neck, that he had left black and blue marks. These marks were evidence that he had abused my mother during his fit of anger. Now, along with my own anger for not being able to come to my mother's aid, whether right or wrong, I had to endure the pain of knowing that David hurt my mother while my father stood outside her door "letting" it happen.

My mind shot back a short time before, and I envisioned the scene when David's brother, Mark, had come home and found his wife in bed with another man. The man Mark caught his wife with was a mutual friend of theirs. In his shock and fury, Mark strangled his wife. She was dead. He had killed her.

Afterwards, he placed her body in the trunk of his car and drove to his brother's house. When he got there, he asked David to come out to the car. Mark confessed to David that he had killed his wife and asked him to help him get rid of the body. Instead, David, being the good police officer, convinced his brother to turn himself in which led to his being arrested. Appearing in court with a plea of insanity, Mark received a five-year prison term.

Shifting back to the scene that transpired in my mother's bedroom, I asked myself, "Would David kill my mother?" I wanted to run and to keep on running until there was no more land on the earth to cover. I had no place to go. Instead, I spent hours rocking on my bed and praying I would not release my own screams that were begging for me to shout. How could my father allow another man, anyone in fact, to beat his wife? Why didn't he protect her? What had being a police officer been all about if he couldn't protect his own family? I didn't get it.

I asked myself over and over again, "Who were these people?" "How did they come to have such a hold over my parents?" My parents should have been able to walk away from Irene and David and get away from them. Why didn't they? As my heart pounded, the sounds in my ears were getting louder and louder. I wanted answers. None would come. Even though I did not know if I would ever have my answers, this was certainly not the right time to ask any questions.

I was learning very early in life to hate men. I did not trust them. Even though I did date some during this time, I was not successful in finding someone to comfort me the way that I needed to be comforted. What I was really looking for was my "dashing knight" to show up on his "white horse" and whisk me away from the dysfunctional life I was living. Those I dated, though, had desires of their own: physical desires. It seemed that they all had one thing in common, and many times I would have to remove their hands from exploring where they ought not to have been.

When I was twenty-two, something traumatic happened to me that would change my life even more. Troubled by the stresses and anxieties I was experiencing in my life, my subconscious was wishing to escape. I had wandered outside in the darkness of the night. I remember the aura of the steps of the library about a block away from our home and the wetness of the light-falling rain. The dog did not bark as I opened the gate leading me to the back door of the house. The dog did not bark when I had struggled to find the hidden key that would open the door when I returned home.

In the fog of awakening at dawn, terror swallowed me up whole. My hair was wet; my nightgown was wet and dirty. The mud was still moist under the sheets I laid on. I did not understand what was happening, and I doubled over as I tried to stand. My head was spinning and, as I struggled to the bathroom down the hall, I could feel extreme pain throughout my whole body.

After vomiting and cleaning myself up, I noticed the bruises on my breast and arms. My pelvic region shot darts of pain. More traumas were to follow as I began to realize I was a victim of rape. I had been sleepwalking and I did not even remember who had violated me. I mustered up courage to call in sick from work, and I hid in the security of my bed for the rest of the day. Fear put another helping on my plate as I was now constantly looking over my shoulders when I ventured outside the house. Was someone watching me?

I did not wear my hearing aid to bed at night. If there were any words spoken around this event when taking place, I did not hear them. At the dinner table that night, my father made a remark that "someone had left the house during the night." He looked right at me. It took all the strength I had not to fall apart and expose my strong desire to scream!

I kept silent—again. I was beside myself when I learned my father knew I had left the house and he did not come after me. He did not try to stop me. He did not protect me. He had not protected me again! I never told anyone about this night, until almost twenty years later. When I did, I crumbled. It was a very sad time for me.

I turned to my guitar. My guitar would become my best friend. When I wanted to cry or when I was angry, I played my guitar. It was also nice to have an outlet when I wanted to share rare feelings of happiness. I expressed my emotions in the songs I sang.

After the rape, I needed a real friend. The twelve-string guitar I played was my confidant, a true and trusted friend for many years to come.

Despite the deep depression I now fought to keep at bay, I drowned myself in the comfort of my singing and with the music made with Chloe' and Aude as we sang together. For the time being, singing was the only way any of us could disquiet the hidden emotions we all had. Music allowed us to empty our hearts of any ill feelings we had going on inside us and allowed us to replace them with the good feelings that came from the songs we sang and from the people we entertained.

At the deepest point in my life, music also allowed me to find the strength to overcome my past. It helped me refill my heart with new memories. It was not hard for people to discern which songs I related to, and I loved being able to make them feel what I was feeling. Music was a good healing outlet for me. Music gave me a reason to continue wanting to live, and it helped me to keep searching to find who I really was and who I could be. It gave me the tools I needed to survive.

# CHAPTER SEVEN

## The Stucco House and The 4th Floor Walk Up

The landlords sold the green house we had been renting for the past eight years...wait for it...we had to move again! This time, we were moving to a house my parents were now purchasing. My grandparent, Edith's parents, had lent them the necessary down payment to secure a loan with the bank to buy the house. A week later, my grandmother, was calling our home and demanding the money back. My grandmother never phoned us so this meant she was not joking. She wanted her money back and she wanted it NOW!

Apparently my parents must have found a way to pay my grandmother because she did not have to call back to remind them again. We had gone to visit them a few days later and it was then, probably, that my mother gave her parents the money they had loaned her—every "red cent." Had she paid them back with pennies?

The stucco house was much smaller than the one we had just been living in. David and Irene's children were getting older now and they opted to stay in their own home on the weekends. They were either dating or active in sports. Even with the smaller space, David and Irene showed themselves at our door every weekend anyway!

David and Irene's sons, Christopher, Matthew, Collin and my half-brother Hugh, all played varsity football for their high school teams. On the weekends, their teams were playing, David, Edith, some of my siblings and I would go and sit in the metal bleachers to cheer for them and their teams.

East Longmeadow was still a small town at this time. When sitting together on the benches appearing to belong with one another like a "family," many of the older folks sitting in around us would stare at us. I am sure they were trying to figure out who the man was that was sitting with my mother. Some may have known David and knew he was not our father, or my mother's husband. Others possibly wondered why David was coming to the games with my mother. There were many questions about the connection between the two of them. I had them, many of my siblings had them, relatives had them and the townspeople had them, too. What all of us folks did not have, were the answers to these questions.

Irene and my father occupied their time, when not in the bedroom, of course, working on their puzzles they put together at the table in our finished basement. Here they would smoke their cigarettes and drink their beers. Often, I would be playing my guitar when they came down to the basement and I continued playing all the while trying to block out their presence.

Edith and David continued their nightly ritual and busying themselves with conversation while enjoying their tea and toast with strawberry jam. They also spent some of their time playing the guitars they had purchased while we were still living at the green house. My mother would sing as David picked at the various notes he was learning. I can still see my mother laying her long fingers on the strings as she tried to master the chords on the neck of her green guitar.

When we moved to the stucco house, I was twenty-two. My sisters, Chloe', Aude and Mildred, were still living at home, also. Chloe' and Mildred shared the bedroom nearest my father's bedroom. Aude and I shared the bedroom across the hall from my mother. Down the hall about the middle of all the bedrooms was our bathroom.

The first Christmas at our new home was probably one of the more pleasant holidays I remember celebrating. On Christmas Eve, Gerard received a phone call from someone in Florida informing him that his mother, Esther, was "dying." No discussions were needed. My father got in our car and immediately drove down to Florida so he could tell her his "goodbyes."

It seemed that when Esther was lonely or in need of attention, she often cried "wolf" and let everyone think she was going under. Phone calls, letters or cards of well wishes would temporarily ward off this loneliness and she would soon be feeling better again. Like other times before this one, after Gerard spent the week visiting with Esther, he then would come back home again. It was always calmer around the home while he was gone and we often wished that he would just stay in Florida but he always came back. Nevertheless, even if he was gone for just a few days, it would be a much welcomed reprieve for all of us.

During the following summer, Esther came up from Florida to visit us. I had not seen her since the time she spent with us at the slightly larger home we had moved to when I was about six years old. She looked the same to me, just a little bit older. During her stay with us, we helped her "heal" from whatever ailment she came to us with. She gained sixteen pounds while staying with us and eating at our home.

On the night before Esther was to leave to go back to her home, she came downstairs to where my siblings and I had been sitting and watching television. She had been talking with my dad in his bedroom. We all, at one time or another, had our turns sitting at length in my father's room as he told us his "sob stories." It was now Esther's turn. He was her son. She probably played a big part in formulating the person my father turned out to be and probably was the cause of many of his emotional dramas. Listening to him in his drunkard state gave her an opportunity to taste what we dealt with on a daily basis.

After a long while, she came down the stairs. She was definitely saddened by what he had told her. My grandmother approached us and asked us, "If one of us could please go upstairs and tell our father we loved him?" For what seemed like eternity, my sisters and I stared at each other. I could see panic forming behind the pupils of their eyes. There was silence.

I felt sorry for my father and now I was feeling sorry for my grandmother to have to see her son in such a depressed state of mind. I said I would go up. When I got to my father's room, he was drunk and weeping like a baby. He was devastated that "none of his babies loved him!" When I tried to tell him I loved him, he waved his hand and shooed me away. He told me to leave. As I leaned down to place a kiss on his forehead, he turned his head. There was nothing I could say or do. I closed the door behind me and left him drowning in his sorrows.

At this time, I was still working at the marketing company, going on four years now. I was dating a young fellow. After a while, I learned that Matthew had cancer. He was leaving as he wanted to return to his hometown in Minnesota before he died. I was beside myself, as I had pictured in my mind that someday we would have gotten married.

After Matthew left, I looked for comfort from my guitar. I wrote a song around this and shared the music with my family. Basically, the response I got from Edith was, "Get over it. There are other fishes in the sea!" This is not what I wanted to hear from my mother during this difficult time. I wanted comfort, loving attention that only a "real" mother could provide. I didn't hold my breath. None was given. The rest of the family listened when I sang my new song, but kept any thoughts they had rolling in their heads to themselves.

Shaking off the shock of the sudden change in direction my life would now take, I tried to start the new day with a positive attitude. Instead of harboring resentments or feeling sorry for myself, I started my mornings off by saying, "Good morning" to everyone. I was trying to generate and maintain a chipper and upbeat spirit. The new me! I can still see my mother's quizzical look as she asked me, "What was ailing me!" Chipper and upbeat were not happening today! The bitterness in my mother's tone of voice told me I had work to do as I was not going to be able to focus on being positive today. I needed to focus on getting ready for work even though I wanted to stay in my bed and die.

My parents loved to play cards. Many of my siblings also had a great love for cards.

Every day after getting out of work, we played a game of cards when we got home while supper was cooking. After we ate supper, we played cards again. After these games, we would retreat to the living room and watch television. My mother often kept her fingers busy while she knitted a sweater or worked on some other knitting project she had going on. David smoked his cigarettes as he watched my mother and some television. My sisters and I tried to keep our eyes on the television so as not to draw attention to ourselves. Mildred would be flipping through magazines and cutting out coupons for free brochures at the back of any magazines we had laying around the house.

Tension was mounting as my father's drinking was beginning to cause us to voice our anger. While he had spent the years drinking his life away and while he was aging, he had not noticed that his children were growing up themselves. In June, when it was Edith's birthday, I had given my father some money to purchase a cake for this occasion before leaving for work in the morning. When I got home from work, there was no cake in sight and Gerard was so drunk he could hardly stand on his feet. It was not going to take a "rocket scientist" to figure out what he had done with the "cake" money I had given him.

Chloe', my father and I were at the table discussing the "no cake" issue and it was not going too well. As Chloe' sat at the table glaring at Gerard for thinking only about his needs, she grew angrier by the minute. Suddenly and not the least expected, Gerard's face changed and he began looking like an evil villain ready to pounce on his soon to be victim. "Chloe', he said to her, "you don't love me do you?" Without skipping a heartbeat, Chloe' replied that "he had not given her anything to love him for!" Oh boy, this was not a good idea! My father jumped up from his seat and hauled off and smacked her across the face with all his might. I was sure she would have a broken neck from his blow or, at least, have a whiplash as a result of this. I had imagined that World War III was about to begin. To my surprise though, instead of having a long drawn out battle, my father left the table and retreated to his bedroom. I then left the house to purchase the cake myself. The familiar gut wrenching feeling was gnawing at my stomach again!

When my mother returned home, we did the birthday celebration thing and I left right afterward. I had gone to see my brother Gabriel and his wife Rhonda who had moved back to Springfield after my brother finished his term with the Marines. I told them about the incident at home, and I really did not want to go back there. The situation had just gotten uglier and I was stressed to the max. I realized that living at home was becoming too much for me to bear. My "emotional plate" was full! I'd had enough. My mind started to race as I tried to come up with the remedy and plan for my escape.

There was a newspaper on the table and I picked it up to look at the listings for apartment rentals. I did see an apartment I thought I could afford, and I called to make an appointment to see the place. It was on the fourth floor of the apartment building and it had three large rooms surrounding the small kitchenette and bathroom. The good thing about this apartment was the location. It was just down the street from Gabriel and Rhonda's house. Louisa and her family lived across the street from them; however, sadly, we were not speaking to each other at this time.

After meeting with the landlord the next day, I put money down to secure the place until July 1st. Since my mother also worked for the same marketing company as

I was working for, it was there I opted to tell her my news about my moving. I figured this way, she couldn't do any screaming. Not in the office anyway.

My heart was pounding as I approached her desk. I told her I had found an apartment and that I would be leaving in a couple of weeks. I explained that Gerard was her husband and she could choose to put up with his abuse and his drinking if she wanted too. I, on the other hand, was not going to live around the continued abuses or around my father's drinking anymore. I was moving on. I was not married to him. Edith asked me to let her tell Gerard that I was leaving. No problem there, I was fine with this request.

After I walked away from her desk and having made my intentions clear, Edith spoke to a few of her women co-workers about my decision to leave home and spread my wings. She wagered "bets" to see how many weeks it would be before I came back home with my "tail" between my legs. She guessed it would be six weeks. This was not going to happen. I vowed that I would never move back to live with my parents ever again.

That night, my mother told Gerard about my plans to move out. He made a phone call to Florida to speak with his mother. I can still hear his words to her. "He could not believe one of his babies was leaving because of him!" He was gone two days later. He had gone to spend some time with his mother in Florida.

While he was gone, I busied myself preparing to move into my new place. Chloe' was going to be starting nursing school in the fall, a few months from now, and I told my mother I was taking her with me. I felt she would need a peaceful environment to concentrate on her schooling. With the event that transpired around the cake issue, I did not want to leave her behind. I was afraid that Gerard would now start to take his anger out on her when he returned. She gladly accepted my offer. Two and a-half weeks before my twenty-fourth birthday, Chloe' and I had packed up, unpacked and were now enjoying the peace we were experiencing in our new home.

Our leaving home was hard on my father. He opted to stay with his mother for a while. When his mother could no longer put up with his drinking, she sent him to see his sister, Geraldine, in California. After having to deal with my father's drinking for several months, Geraldine had enough, too, and put him on a plane back our way on Christmas Eve.

Chloe' and I had gone to my parents' house on Christmas Eve. I was anxious. I was not sure how my father would welcome me. As I glanced at him standing at the top of the stairs, I could see that he was drunk and this took away any ideas going on in my head that he would be open for communicating with me. We did the "open the present thing" and I left right afterwards. I only saw my father once more after this night.

Chloe' decided that she was going to change her classes of interest and was going to start the new term at a different college. She would be living in a dorm now and was going to be moving out of our apartment. She was making new friends and was finding peace with her changes. This was okay with me. This would be a new experience for her and I was excited at the opportunity to be living by myself.

I continued to play my guitar and I was writing more of my own music. Music helped to release many of the emotions I held inside. Having developed a spiritual need, music allowed me to strengthen this need. I tried very hard to change my attitude about life. I did not want to become like my parents and, if I was going to be different from them, there were changes I needed to make.

I had always been told that "God loved me." At this time in my life, I thought that maybe it was to God I should give my heart. I set out to explore this avenue only to find myself at a dead end. I just did not feel God wanted me. I was certain He did not need me either.

I began realizing that I had spent most of my life trying to please others, trying to be good and trying not to cause problems for anyone. Well, I reasoned that being "good" had gotten me nowhere. Therefore, at this point in time, I decided I was going to change this and I crossed over to the dark side. I would look for avenues that would make me happy. I did not care what it would cost me or what the consequences would be for ill decisions I would make. It was time to make me happy! Party-time!

Changes continued developing around me and I was accepting that my wanting to be part of a close and loving family was not going to happen. In fact, there were few siblings left remaining to interact with at the home base (my parents' house) at this point. In just a few short years since living at the green house, our family circle had shifted from having two parents and seven siblings in our home and it had dwindled to one parent and two siblings.

After graduating from high school, my brother Gabriel and his friend had enlisted in the military. It was during the height of the Viet Nam War. I am thankful that during his four years of service that he never left the borders of the United State. Shortly after completing his boot camp training, Gabriel married his first love, Rhonda. Their first home was just outside the military base where my brother was assigned.

Alan had left home while we were still living in the green house. When he failed to comply with paying my mother his weekly room and board, tension mounted around this issue and he decided he would move. One afternoon, he was just gone. He had run away. Because of this, he never did complete high school and never got his diploma.

After having been away for some time, Alan did make his way back to Springfield. It was not going to be long though before he could not take the pressure in the home and he would leave us again. Eventually Alan married and had children of his own. We did not keep in contact with each other. It would be thirty years before I spoke with him again.

I was never close to my brothers. I wished I had had a relationship with them. Living down the street from Gabriel now, this gave me an opportunity to build on a relationship with him. We shared a common interest. This common factor was drugs.

This would pretty much be the only time we could laugh together. The wedges placed there by the happenings of our past seemed to hide themselves in the clouds around us made by the smoke of the marijuana joints we were puffing.

This was not the type of relationship I had hoped for. These drugs would only lead us down roads that would make us no better than our parents. At this moment, I did not care about my image. Being high allowed me to disappear into a world where there was no pain. It also blocked out of my mind where I had come from, and the life I had lived up to the present time.

Louisa and her husband, Brian, were married and had two children of their own. Even though we were not speaking at this time, I knew that Louisa would be a good mother.

None of the four adults would ever have a chance to play their games with her children.

They would never get a chance to mess with her children whether it would be emotionally or physically. Burning arrows released from her eyes would have penetrated deeply into the muscle of their hearts should they even dare try.

Chloe' was still going to school and was making a new circle of friends. She continued to play her guitar and used her music abilities to embark on a spiritual journey of her own.

Aude and Mildred were still living at home. Aude found employment. At some point, she would buy her own home. She did travel some but really never ventured too far beyond the horizon.

Mildred was still in school and spent her days writing to pen pals whose addresses she obtained from the back of magazines. After a brief and abusive marriage, she obtained a divorce from her husband and returned home to live with my mother, Aude and my father.

Now that the children conceived in the four-way relationship and had gotten older and had started new lives for themselves, my father divorced my mother and they went their separate ways. My mother stayed in the stucco house and my father, as he often did, migrated to Florida to be with his mother.

Gerard spent his time fishing and going out on the ocean with his step-brother Gordon.

To some degree, fishing afforded my father a little peace. However, he never did come back our way to live. He had originally promised Irene that he would be back in two weeks after a short visit with his mother. He had retired from driving truck and was looking for some much needed R & R. As irony would have it, he actually ended up living with one of Irene's friends who was currently living in Florida near my grandmother. Embittered by this betrayal, Irene refused to divorce David. David did move in with my mother, although they never married.

It was under the influence of drugs that I would happen to meet Charlie. Before I knew it, he had moved in with me and was now living in my apartment. Charlie was a musician and spent most of his days playing guitar, preparing himself for gigs he might have lined up. We had many parties at my apartment. Many of Charlie's nephews were constant guest in our home. They had always been close to Charlie growing up and were about the same age as he was. Most importantly, as Charlie himself did, they too enjoyed good music; good drinks and they loved a good party!

Just as I could see my parents reaping consequences for mistakes they had made, I was about to face the music to the same "fiddler" they had danced to. Oh dear!

# CHAPTER EIGHT

## The House at the Bottom of the School Hill

I recently moved back to my old hometown of East Longmeadow, Massachusetts, where I had lived before moving to the Green House. Charlie moved here with me. I was twenty-seven years old and I was pregnant. We recently moved into the new apartment after needing to seek alternate living quarters due to our newest situation. We had been living in an "adult only" apartment complex and management did not favor children living in the building. Charlie and I had run into Irene at a local restaurant and after she heard we needed a place to live, she offered her empty apartment to us.

This newer apartment was in Irene's house. We would be on the second floor. One floor below us was where my half-brothers and Irene lived. My brother Alan was living there at this time also. Irene's husband David was currently living with my mother Edith.

My father Gerard had gone to visit his mother in Florida. She felt she was "dying" and my father opted to stay with her until she got better or passed on. However, my grandmother did not die and my father moved in with Irene's friend Sylvia after he divorced my mother. Sylvia had been wintering in Florida for some time now and her place was near where my grandmother lived. Displeased with Gerard's decision to stay in Florida, Irene refused to give David a divorce so he could marry my mother as planned. This did not make for peaceful conditions for me or Charlie for that matter.

Even after having been away from my family and living on my own for the past three years, I came to realize after a few days that nothing had changed. I had forgotten all the rules to the games the four adults played, and now I had them staring me in the face again. My father's decision to stay with Sylvia only added another player to these games. Irene's mood swings had not gone away and it seemed that she looked for ways to make my life difficult. All too late, I realized, I had made a huge mistake moving into this apartment.

It was eerie, at first, to be living in the house where I had spent much time off and on during weekends after the four-way relationship between my father, mother, Irene and David had started. Once Charlie and I had settled into our apartment, memories of my yesteryears at this house started to release themselves from the cobwebs of my memory.

The house was a good hundred years old and was sitting on a very small parcel of land. The front yard was just a tad bit smaller than the backyard. The two-car garage held the bicycles and sleds used considerably by

Irene and David's children and later by my siblings and me when we visited.

The garage also held a tool that I found much joy in using. It was an old push mower which featured a wooden neck that supported the handles you held on to when pushing the mower. I loved watching the blades rotate as I pushed the mower through the growing grass in the back yard. I remember the smell emitted when the blades of grass gave off their scent as they fell limply on the ground underneath.

The front yard did not need to be mowed often. Any grass growing in this area never stood around long enough to need mowing as the shoes of eleven lively children was going to trample down any life that appeared under their soles. I was very careful to avoid mowing down the large rhubarb plants that grew on the corner of the house as you came off the back steps. Oh, the dread that would come my way if Irene could not make her "rhubarb" pies! I made a mental note to always mow around the patch of rhubarb.

Flowering snapdragons, yellow, and pink, and orange tiger lilies grew on the edges of the property. Purple and yellow johnny-jump-ups played peek-a-boo amongst the mixture of foliage that did not need much attention.

A tree towards the end of the property shaded the white lilies of the valley that grew around the base of the trunk. Branches and leaves from the top of the tree growing on the land below were strong and we used to hold on to these branches for balance and support when we lowered ourselves down the steep slump onto the grass behind the large brick church. This was a short cut that got us where we needed to go a lot faster. Were we in a hurry?

It was hard to imagine that eleven children played in this yard when we were younger. When I look at this yard today, it hardly seemed large enough to park a car. I was amazed at how my perception had changed as I aged, and as time went passing by.

There was a field to the left side of Irene's house. In the spring and summertime, nature painted bouquets of flowers for all of us to admire. My favorite flowers growing in this field were the white daisies. Our hands held clumps of daisies as we pulled off each white petal one at a time and repeated the old childhood rhymes, "He loves me, and He loves me not!" Black-eyed su-san's with deep yellow petals, bright yellow dandelions and wild purple and white violets grew around these larger flowers. In the fall after much of the prettiness had disappeared in the field and the colors faded off the stems that held them, milkweeds made their ap-pearance and remained to wear the snow that would soon clothe them.

On the other side of this field was a brown house. An elderly woman with pure white hair worn in a bun on the back of her head had lived there. I had not visited her often, but remember a time when I had. I can still picture in my memory her smile adorned with deep blood red lipstick. She painted her cheeks with a stroke of red rouge to give them some color. She was pale and this made the colors stand out even more on her face. She offered me a treat from her oven. I accepted this relishing treat with grace. My joy did not last long, however, as I noticed some bugs enjoying this treat ahead of me.

Not long after, an ambulance came and took her away. I remember the emergency crew brining her down the outer staircase of her home strapped in a stair chair. After this day, I never saw her again. Soon after she left, people came and tore her house down. It was there one minute and gone the next.

The new owners of the property turned her land into a large parking lot for the brick church below us. People coming for church services thereafter on the weekends filled the parking lot with their cars.

Our apartment was identical to Irene's place downstairs. It had two bedrooms, a kitchen with a pantry and a very large living room. At one point in time, someone removed the wall of a former bedroom and enlarged the living room. Our bathroom held an old claw foot tub, which was still shining after all the years of use.

All the rooms in the house except for the master bedroom were painted a dull mint-green color. The master bedroom was a deep bluish gray that reminded me of the color of the uniforms worn during the Civil War.

Charlie was a musician and had gigs every now and then where he played his music. At some point, he had gotten a job working with his friend Phillip delivering bread. Around the due date for our baby to be born, he had hurt his back at work and was now recuperating from his injury.

I was still working for a marketing company. I had worked at my position for the last ten years, almost to the date from when I had started working before I had to leave. As I got closer to the due date, I left my employment. I needed to use any remaining time before the baby was born to prepare myself for motherhood, and get things ready around the home for the baby. We were soon going to be welcoming our baby into the world and into our home. I was excited!

I wallpapered one of the walls in the spare bedroom with a circus print covered with colorful tents and baby animals. The bright colors of yellow, orange and browns seemed to give the room a touch of comfort.

The crib bar held a musical mobile that would spin green baby frogs and pink baby pigs as it was spinning around. When wound up, it played the tune from the song, "It's a Small World." Hanging from the ceiling above the crib was a large yellow and black bumblebee. It had white wings. The bumblebee dangled from the ceiling on an elastic band. After releasing the band when pulled, you could watch the bumblebee spin around and flap its wings. As it bounced around flapping its wings up and down, rattle sounds from within the belly of the bumblebee played its music. Our baby was going to love this!

Since this was my first baby, I was apt to be nervous. Would my hearing impairment prevent me from being able to hear when my baby cried? When it needed me? Or when it was hurting? Would my own upbringing stand in the way of my being able to love and nurture the baby as a mother should? Although I was determined to show this child every ounce of love I could offer, I will admit, I was scared. I did not want to fail. I wanted to be a good mother.

Charlie on the other hand, already had two children from his first marriage and was not as excited as I thought he would be about the new baby. After all, he had already been through the "pregnancy and baby entering the world" stuff twice, as I was often reminded when I got excited about something happening to my body or as the baby developed. His words seemed harsh to me. His not wanting to walk with me during the different stages of my pregnancy was a great disappointment to me.

I looked at this child as a precious gift from God. Not everyone around me felt the same though. Charlie felt trapped in some way and, at first, felt that I should get an abortion. I remember telling him that I would have this baby with or without him. Already I was feeling the life within the walls of my abdomen and there was no way I was going to terminate this life. He could leave if he wanted to but the baby was staying!

An aunt asked me after I shared the exciting news about the baby with her, "What would my grandmother say?" She then proceeded to ask me, "if I was going to give the baby up for adoption?" Other family members and some of my friends were upset that we did not get married when I learned I was pregnant.

Charlie's hesitation to support the pregnancy at the beginning when I told him the news alerted me to the fact that he did not love me. Yet, I did not want to fail in my relationship with him and opted to stay with him. I was going to give it my best shot and do everything I could to make our relationship work.

I spent many hours listening to Charlie as he played with various other musicians. I did not particularly care for the bar scene, but I did want to support Charlie's efforts to fulfill his dreams of "hitting it big" as a singer. Since I had a dislike to using alcohol because of my father's abuse of the substance, I did not drink. When I learned I was with child, I chose never to let alcohol touch my lips. I immediately stopped smoking marijuana and would no longer allow others to smoke this substance in my home. I had a baby to consider.

Even though I had conceived under the influence of drugs, I was hoping to give the baby a healthy start in life. I had to make positive changes to ensure this new beginning. This did not sit well with Charlie. He felt because I did not want to "party" anymore that he believed I was going to love the baby more than I would love him. The baby was not even here yet and I already perceived we would have problems in the near future. So, no, I did not want to marry Charlie. From this point on, we really did not have anything in common. He continued to focus on his music and I focused on preparing for the arrival of our baby.

I had called my sister Louisa when I learned I was pregnant and she gladly accepted when I asked her to be my birthing coach. Having had two children of her own, and loving them, I asked her to help me. I greatly benefited from her experiences. She spared me no details. Although I knew there was going to be labor pains, Louisa focused on the joys of becoming a mother. Love radiated from her heart and soul as she shared her own joys with me.

Louisa, as she promised, stayed with me until the baby made her appearance into the world. After four days of labor, our daughter finally arrived. Our little princess who we now called Emily Jane was beautiful. Delivered by Cesarean Section, Emily Jane had not had to experience the trauma of squeezing through the birth canal and sported a perfectly round head with just a little peach fuzz for her crown.

Instantly, after the nurses handed my baby to me, I felt a tremendous connection with her. I would never wish to break this connection. I had bonded with her as I carried her, and now that she arrived and was in my arms, nothing and no one was going to take the joy I was feeling away from me. No one was going to hurt her as long as I was around. She would have my protection, my love and my direction. I was determined to be a good mother.

When holding Emily Jane, I couldn't understand how my mother, or any mother for that matter, could carry a baby, bring it into this world and not feel a connection with her child. Even if there is some sort of medical condition like postpartum blues, at some point with medication and therapy, I would hope these women could bond with their child.

For whatever reason or reasons, I do not feel Edith ever bonded with any of her seven children. Something was missing. Irene used to always say that "any woman could have a baby, but not all of them can be mothers." Having babies was not supposed to be a temporary chore to put away after birth. It was a lifelong commitment. I was determined to love my baby and wanted to always be there for her.

Emily Jane became the rays of light shining through my years of shattered dreams. I had a reason to awaken each day. I found myself eager to hear the sounds of my little girl's cry in the morning. To my delight, Emily Jane responded to my presence and greeted me with her smiles. Feeding times, diaper changes, bath times, play times and nap times, moments of silence; all these radiated such joy that it helped to soften anything that would come my way as we faced each new day.

Charlie did not take to being a father very well, although he did love Emily Jane. He feared the responsibilities that came with providing for and then fathering another baby. There were moments I felt he was jealous of the time I spent with our newborn. Even though I tried to include him in our daily routine and show he, too, was important, I could never do enough to assure him of our love.

After Emily Jane was born, Charlie did not feel I loved him. Or, he felt I loved the baby more than I did him. It was true that he was no longer the center of my attention and, for me, he would never again come first in my life. My priority now was getting Emily Jane through the toughest part of her life: the "living it" part! He could join us on this trek or he could continue to drown in self-pity. Either way, Emily Jane was still going to be number one from now on!

It would not be long after Emily Jane was born that Charlie's back was feeling much better. He had gotten a job working in construction. His work schedule took him away from our home for many hours a week. Right on schedule though, when he returned from his shift, he would insert the key to our front door and, after turning the key, he would open the door. As he ascended the stairs, Emily Jane would awaken and was ready to greet her father home from work.

While I fixed Charlie a snack to eat, he held his daughter and used this time to strengthen his bond with her. Even though he never did say it in so many words, he was proud of his baby girl. He read her stories and softly sang to her. This was their time. I was happy that they were off to a good start in their relationship. I had not had a relationship with my father and I wanted Emily Jane to have the opportunity I had missed.

Like her mother and father, Emily Jane loved music. It did not matter what kind of music we played, she just loved listening to music. When Charlie played guitar during the later stage of my pregnancy, I could feel her move with the rhythm of the beat. There were times I had to leave the house to settle her down. I did not always feel like dancing. However, Emily Jane had other ideas of her own. She responded to the music Charlie played and wanted to jump through the walls of my skin and hop right onto the floor and dance the night away!

Many times after she was born, I would sit her in her infant seat on the floor in front of the television set and I would watch her wiggle with delight as she responded to the beat of any music played during the commercials.

After Emily Jane was born, my family did not have a lot of interaction with her. However, after leaving the hospital I did spend a few days recuperating at my mother's home and Edith, Audie and Mildred tended to the baby when she cried. This allowed me a few moments more of needed sleep.

Mildred spent a week with us after Charlie brought us home. She was very helpful to me. I appreciated all her efforts when tending to her niece as I was still healing from the C-section that delivered Emily Jane into the world. Mildred would softly talk to her as she was changing her diapers and then she would bring the baby into my bedroom so I could feed her.

After a week, I was feeling much stronger and could now do more for myself. Mildred went back home and was probably happy to be able to get the rest she needed after spending this time with us! After this week, other than a few visits to the homes of some of our relatives and a couple more visits to grandma's house, this would be the only time my family spent interacting with Emily Jane. On top of any other reason they had for staying away, my family was not fond of Charlie and this made them determined to keep their distance.

Although on the other end of the spectrum, Irene welcomed the few times I brought Emily Jane downstairs for visits. She held her for me as I went to the basement to do a load of laundry. As I watched Irene gently touching my baby's little fingers I was seeing a kinder side of her that I had never witnessed before. Irene seemed to be content when holding Emily Jane and, for few moments, it appeared this provided Irene a temporary dosage of peace.

Even still, I never did leave my daughter with Irene for more than a few minutes at a time. Memories of my past experiences with Irene continued to show their ugly scenes before my eyes and I did not want to give Irene any chances to play games with my newborn.

In the few short months after I had begun living in the apartment above Irene, more memories showed themselves to my presence. Memories about things I had witnessed in the basement. Recently in one of my conversations with Louisa about the "basement," she blurted out a memory she had about something David did in the basement. It brought back to my mind that I, too, had seen him do the same. Although we did not catch him in the act, we both remembered his "smile," and how his victim couldn't get away from him fast enough.

These memories and memories like them will continue to be just that—memories. When I tried to let these horrors out in the past, I would hold back from spilling the beans. These memories make me want to vomit when they try to free themselves from deep storage bins in my mind. These will have to continue to remain hidden secrets for the time being.

What I gleaned from my conversations with Louisa is that what I remembered from events that happened during my youth really had happened and I had not made them up.

When I wondered what might have happened around certain events, talking it out between the two of us and digging into the wells of the past, enabled us to piece together as adults what I am glad we did not know as children. I am glad that these walls cannot talk.

More memories would then come back to me as we talked about the basement. At the bottom of the stairs leading down into the basement, as you turned to the right, there was a heavy door. When you opened the door, there was a hole in the cement floor on the left of the threshold.

During my youth, Irene was always telling me this hole belonged to the "devil." It was the "devil's hole!" She then would add that "if I stepped in it, the devil would grab me and drag me through the hole and take me into hell!" I dreaded having to go down to the basement for any reason. I mean if he (the devil) had an entrance to his home in the basement, then he had to be around somewhere in the basement, too. Right?

Now, years later, I learned that this hole was plain and simply just a "drain hole." Any water that may have entered the basement through the hatchway when it rained or when the snow melted, the water would drain through this hole and be rerouted to the outside of the house. I could not believe it had been a drain hole and nothing more.

When I thought of Irene's comments when I first went back in the basement after moving to this house, I wondered what made Irene want to tell an innocent child such horrible stories. Why did she feel a need to have to scare me? More memories began to escape and I would rush up the stairs to assure my child of my protection. Irene was not going to have any time to try anything evil with my daughter. I did not leave her often and any other visits made after so Irene could see the baby were short.

I was not the only who had a dislike for Irene. Charlie did not care for Irene either. He actually did not have anything good to say about Gerard, David or Edith for that matter. After sharing stories of my past with him, he formed a strong disgusting opinion of them that would never change.

When Irene tried to interfere in our affairs, Charlie did not hold back from loudly declaring his anger. When hearing his comments, Irene did not take this lightly. She managed to find ways to retaliate and throw rocks into my already tensed relationship with Charlie.

For example, once when Charlie purchased a motorcycle, Irene did not want him to park the bike in the driveway. She felt that I was being irresponsible and thought it was wrong for me to even consider riding on a motorcycle. After all, "I had a baby to care for!" "What was I thinking?" I went for ONE ride. It was Charlie's bike. Why was she taking her frustrations out on me? However, Irene could shout all she wanted; she wasn't going succeed in telling Charlie what to do. I didn't care for her trying to tell to me what to do either.

Louisa loved motorcycles and Charlie took her for a short ride on his bike. Irene had a lot to say about this issue also. After all, Louisa had two children. When Irene was done making her thoughts known so "everyone" could hear, it was quiet again. Until the mail arrived a few days later delivering a letter from Irene demanding that we, not Charlie, remove the motorcycle from her yard or we were going to have to find another place to live. For the time being, the motorcycle was going to be parked in the new parking lot next to the house.

Situations like these helped me to understand why my brother Alan had almost nothing to do with me or say to me while he lived just one floor below me. I couldn't understand why he would not come up to see his newest niece. There was nothing I could say that could convince him to make such effort. In theory, I figured he did not want Irene to know or see that he had spent any time with me. He was probably trying to avoid any darts that her bouts of jealous anger would throw at him. I am sure that any conversations he had with Irene around me being the subject were not positive and he kept his distance so that he could continue living at the place he was now calling home. Why would he want to "rock" the boat?

I don't know why Irene thought she could continue to control what I did or what went on in my house. My only guess would be that she felt she could do this as this is what she had always done with our family, which included me!

Charlie and I wanted to have a little get-together with a few couples at our place. Irene put her foot down and was adamant that she did not want a bunch of people in our apartment. After all, these folks would be over her head and she felt that they just might come falling through the floor and end up sitting on her lap downstairs! Who had the imagination this time?

Another vice that Irene was dead set against was having animals in our apartment. Charlie ignored her rights as our property owner to set the rules and regulations for us, as her tenants, to follow. Nevertheless, Charlie who did not take orders from any woman ignored her demands and got himself a puppy. He wanted a puppy and no one, including Irene, was going to tell him he could not have a puppy! End of story? Not quite!

A few days later, we received an eviction notice in our mail box. We now needed to find another place to live! Even though I was angry with Charlie for getting the pup and at Irene for being a royal pain in the butt, I kept silent. My thoughts were never introduced to my lips. However, Charlie did not keep silent! Everyone knew he was angry including the Queen, Irene! Hearing his words filter through the floor was like setting off loaded rockets. His explicit words sent Irene flying through the roof!

Let's just say after this incident that I did my laundry around Irene's schedule. I did not want to run into her on my way down to the basement. I went out of my way to avoid having any contact with her. I think she must have done the same as I did not see much of her after we got our notice. I don't believe either of us wanted to face a blown out confrontation. In other words, World War III! I also did not want the abusive speech coming from Irene and Charlie's mouth (and sometimes mine) to scare Emily Jane and cause her any trauma.

Gut wrenching pains and unhappy memories were like platoons marching around me trying to invade my soul. It felt like I was walking on eggshells (land mines) and had to choose the steps I would take as I had so often done when the adults were moody or when my father was drunk in my younger years.

Irene's escapades and games were frustrating Charlie and he decided he was going to move and he was moving out of state, far away from this woman! He shouted "if I was going with him, I needed to pack!"

I took a few moments to recap my situation. My choices stood clearly before my mind's eyes. One, I could stay behind with Emily Jane and continue to live around the abuse and Irene's control issues. Or two, I could swallow the fears that engulfed me as I wondered what leaving and moving away would bring my way if I left with Charlie. I must admit, neither of these was going to be a good choice. Nevertheless, I did choose and decided Emily Jane and I would be moving with Charlie.

Therefore, when Emily Jane was nine months old, we set about making plans to move. Emotionally, I was feeling I had been thrown through the wringer during the past twelve months I had been living in the apartment above Irene and with Charlie. I was hoping the move would free me from the walls of the apartment and from Irene. Tense moments mounted over the next few weeks. This freedom would not come fast enough for me.

Mixed feelings developed in my mind as I packed our home. I was angry with Irene for allowing her ugliness to penetrate into my home and family. I was angry at Charlie for not being able to keep his mouth shut. Why couldn't he keep quiet as I had done when growing up around her and having had to deal with her crazy mood swings?

I meditated and passed the pros and cons of this move around in my head. I came to the conclusion that moving with Charlie was going to be the right choice. I really did need to get away from the games and the people who played them. I did not want to be their "game piece" anymore! Soon, we would be moving into our new place and I would be far away and out of the reach of all the adults! At twenty seven years of age and rehashing all the "games" I had lost over these years, I decided change might be for the best. This was a good decision. Well, at least, I was hoping it would be.

# CHAPTER NINE
## The A-Frame Chalet

*O*ur new place was a small A-Frame chalet tucked in between the tall green trees that grew nearby. It had a little kitchenette, a living room and two small bedrooms downstairs. The bathroom did not have a claw-foot tub like all the other homes I had lived in. This place had a shower. I had trepidations.

I had never taken a "real" shower before. Even though we were supposed to take showers after our gym classes in school, I do not know too many of the girls in my class who actually took one. I know I never did. Who wanted to get naked in front of other girls? Not me! I was far too self-conscious for that.

A new experience awaited me as I readied myself for bed. I nervously stepped into the shower. I had to examine the plumbing system. I did not even know how to turn the water on. It was not hard to figure out. Hot water, cold water and the thing-a-ma-jig that you pulled out to route the water to the shower head. I got it! Aaaaahhhhh! I quickly learned that you should always remember to check the running water temperature before getting underneath the shower head!

It was an overwhelming experience for me to have the water coming down on me from over my head. I was nervous about getting water in my ears. My mom had instilled a paranoid fear in me that I would get an ear infection, and would go completely deaf if this were to happen. Once I got used to the newness of this idea, I came to enjoy taking showers over taking baths in the tub. I also liked the fact that showers can cut down on water usage. While I was in the shower a thought came to my mind. How would I give Emily Jane her baths? Then, I came up with a sure solution. The kitchen sink was just the right size for my little one and it was going to work out just fine!

Again, I had the overwhelming task of unpacking boxes and making our place look and feel like a home. While I focused on this challenge, Emily Jane did some exploring of her own. Despite all the boxes stacked up around her, she managed to navigate her walker around any open floor space she could find. Before long, we found some of her toys and she busied herself playing in the playpen while I put away household items.

Charlie kept busy, too. He immediately went to work setting up his music equipment and going about his routine of tuning his guitar and plugging it into his amplifier. He was in his own little world, and was not distracted by the fact that I could have used an extra pair hands to help me put things away or an extra set of eyes to help me keep an eye on Emily Jane. At least for the time being, he kept himself out of my way and didn't need me to help him with anything. Being useful was not his first, middle or last name.

The slanted walls on the main floor of the A-frame made it difficult for Charlie to fit all his equipment squarely against the walls and adjustments needed to be made. Some of his speakers would have to be stored in the basement in the storage area outside the bedrooms. Awwwww!

It was the beginning of November when we moved, and the ski season was just around the corner. The employees at the local ski resort kept busy getting ready for opening day. Snow was being made with snowmaking equipment. These snowmaking "guns" ran all during the night and left inches of fresh snow on the ski trails that were soon to be covered with skiers.

I would soon learn that this man-made snow, as good as it would be for skiers and business, was not going to be good for everyone. Often during the night, the wind would blow snow from these "guns" off the mountain and onto our cars. Since we lived just a short distance from the mountain, scraping snow off the car windshield would become a morning ritual for us. In other words, it would not be good for me as I would be the one needing to get up a little earlier and do everything else I had to do before I went out to scrape snow off the car windows!

One of the first things we had to do after we were done unpacking, was to secure employment. Charlie was interested in getting night bookings at the local lodges and clubs. We agreed that I would find a daytime job, and he would watch Emily Jane while I worked. With my work experience, it did not take me long to acquire a front desk position at the base lodge of the ski resort. The economy was a little different at this hide-a-way town, and it did not offer the city wages I had previously made. However, it was a job and it generated money that enabled us to get supplies we needed.

Shortly after I started my new job, Charlie began complaining that he was not able to practice his "sets" and ready himself for "gig's as Emily Jane was demanding too much of his time and attention. Really, welcome to fatherhood! With an active child around, he couldn't concentrate on his music and wanted me to do something about it. He firmly let me know he did not want to watch her anymore while I was at work. Since it was my job that generated actual money, I needed to keep my job at the mountain. Not having other family members around to help and not knowing anyone in the area yet, I needed to scout out daycare providers a.s.a.p. So, I spent the next couple of nights checking the local paper for suitable options while Charlie watched TV or played his guitar. Hmmm! Did you guess I was making groaning sounds again? You bet!

In time, I was able to find a childcare provider that I was comfortable with about ten miles away toward the center of a nearby town. It was in the completely opposite direction that I needed to be going to get to work. Of, course! This made life a little more stressful for me.

With traffic going into town after the mountain closed for the night, it took me longer to get home after picking up Emily Jane. Charlie would not help. It was "not his thing!" With all the extra gas and childcare fees, my paycheck got smaller and smaller. I often wondered if working was really helping us to get ahead financially. We all know the answer to this question, don't we?

Getting home after it got dark each night was taking its toll on me. I was working fifty-five hours a week. I was traveling to and from the sitter, and then to work and back. I came home to cook, clean and take care of an active child. I was burning out. I found myself wanting to get to bed early after our daughter bedded down for the night.

My going to bed early was not sitting well with Charlie. He was bursting with energy. After having been home alone all day, and having nothing to do but play his guitar, he was ready for some you know—"action." In other words, he wanted my full attention. When I went to bed early, Charlie felt "neglected." What did he mean when he said "he was feeling neglected?" He had to be kidding!

I could tell from the messes left behind in each room what Charlie's day had been like. I knew what he had to eat, if he took a shower, if he watched television or if he just played his guitar. If I asked Charlie to help around the house at night or on my days off, he would remind me that I was the one who "opted not to have an abortion!" He had told me from the start of my pregnancy that "if I had the baby, the baby would be my responsibility!" In other words, all this extra work I had on my plate, in his mind, was not because of his laziness, but because I had a baby. Cleaning up after him was another full time job for me. Nagging him for his help was fruitless.

I looked forward to any night that he had a playing gig. This meant I could go to bed when Emily Jane was sleeping, and I would not have to hear him complain. Until, he started whining about wanting me to go with him when he played out. If I didn't go with him, he felt I was not supporting his efforts to become a rock star. I had already been helping him load up his equipment, bring in his equipment, help him set up his equipment and now he wanted me to arrange for someone to stay with Emily Jane, so I could be with him. Give me a break!

Well, I put my foot down. This wasn't going to happen. First of all, I was not going to leave our baby with a stranger in a strange town. Secondly, I wasn't giving up what little time I had with my daughter so he could have an ego trip in front of a microphone. This added stress to our already troubled relationship. Not only was Charlie feeling like he was not the number one person in my life and that he did not feel that he was loved, but he now added that I wasn't being supportive. Oh well, I'm sorry he felt this way but, too bad, get over it and grow up!

One night, Charlie came home from playing a gig and was all depressed because there were not many people at the lodge to hear him play his sets. He was a good musician so he did not understand why his gig had not attracted a larger crowd. We found out that another guitarist and longtime favorite singer was in the area and playing in a lodge down the street. When he played in the area, he packed the house. Hence, this is where all the people had gone. Charlie started telling me that he was "just as good as this other guitarist" and he didn't understand "why he couldn't get a larger following when he played." What did he think I could do about this? Was he thinking this was my fault, too?

Anyways, he carried on and did this song and dance about how he was "not good enough for Emily and me," and that "he felt we could do better." He felt "he should leave us and that we would be better off without him." I started feeling like I was living with my father all over again, and it was reminding me of all the sob stories I had had to listen to when he was drunk. Well right now, Charlie had my attention. I was listening. So, hurry up already. I wanted to go back to sleep. His whining was driving me crazy. To help him make a decision, I went upstairs, got a couple of trash bags, and started packing his clothing. I told him to leave if he felt he really wanted to do so. As you would think, all the whining made Charlie tired and eventually he fell asleep.

Let's think about this for a moment. He was able to sleep in until he wanted to get up. He had a personal cook and housecleaner. He got to play his guitar all day without any distractions. And, as added bonuses, he got my paycheck and free sex! I had mixed feelings about the idea of him leaving for a minute or two, then a sense of relief came over me when I realized how much more time and energy I would have if he actually left.

I knew Charlie wasn't going anywhere. Just as I thought, he was still there in the morning when I got up. Why wouldn't he be? Other than the lack of money part, he had it made. When he got up later the next morning, he started recapping our conversation from the night before. He was now whining, because he "could not believe I was willing to let him walk out the door!" I was never going to be a winner with Charlie.

Once in a while when he earned money playing out, he had this "post-gig" routine he did after he got paid. He would take us to the nearest city and rent a room at a hotel. Here he would draw himself a bath and soak as he read magazines and drank his beers. Later, we would order pizza and Emily Jane and I would go to bed while he stayed up watching television. If there were any funds left over, he used what was remaining to upgrade his music equipment. He always needed some new strings or something for his PA system. His wish list was never ending. Then, we went back to the real world and the A-frame chalet. Are we having fun yet?

I had gone to bed early one night and I heard Charlie screaming my name. I irritably got out of bed and went running up the stairs. What could all this commotion be about in the middle of the night? I thought he might have hurt himself. When I found him, my sleepy eyes could see that he was not bleeding and that he didn't have any broken bones. His reason for waking me up had better be good!

Charlie took me outside. He wanted to show me something. I was clueless and did not know what to expect. I thought that maybe a UFO had landed or something to the likes of this. No, that wasn't it. He led me to the side of the A-frame, and it was here he showed me some BEAR TRACKS in the snow! I don't know what he was thinking, but it was the middle of the night, it was cold outside, and he had awakened me. Did he really think I was going to be thrilled to be up, and be all goo goo ga ga over the bear tracks? He didn't win any gold stars from me this night! I guarantee this was a fact! I still do not know what he had been doing outside that night in the first place? It remains a mystery to this day like most of the other questions I had asked myself throughout my lifetime.

Shortly thereafter, it was getting closer to the holiday season. Charlie wanted all of us to go into the woods to pick out a tree. You know, like you see in all the family movies that come out at this time of year. Charlie wanted to involve himself with family stuff? Okay, I was willing. I dressed Emily Jane in her yellow snowsuit with her hat, mittens and little boots. We followed Charlie into the woods behind our chalet. I was not smiling as I had no reasons to be smiling. I was not happy. I had to go outside into the woods where, amongst other things, it was COLD! Did Charlie really think I was going to be enjoying this trek after the "bear thing" a few nights before? I could not understand how any man, in this case, Charlie, who had a head on his shoulders and a brain, could come up with such a stupid idea! Right about now, my having moved out of state and into this A-frame chalet did not feel like a good choice. Then, I began thinking how I was not looking much smarter than Charlie right now. Here I was in the middle of the woods looking for "our" special tree with Emily Jane and Charlie! I just had this bad feeling that instead of finding "our" tree, we would more likely cut down a tree that had a BEAR somewhere IN IT! So no, no, noooooooo, I was not feeling any smarter than Charlie at this moment!

Not too long after this trek in the woods, Emily Jane turned one year old. It was snowing, but this did not seem to bother her. The heat kept the floors warm and the rooms toasty. She was not the least bit troubled by the fifty feet of snow outside! She did not have to shovel it. This was something I had to add to my list of things to do when it snowed.

Emily Jane was healthy, happy and adjusting to the life around her. Even though we did not have great television reception at our house, she had plenty to do. Entertainment would come in the form of books, puzzles, music, walks, playing outdoors and from mom and dad.

One night during one of the worse snowstorms that winter, Emily Jane was tired and went to bed earlier than usual. Later when checking on her before heading to bed myself for the night, I could feel the heat from her body as I entered the bedroom. I touch her forehead, and then I panicked. She was HOT! I knew I had to get her to the clinic and to a doctor fast!

I called the clinic and was told to bring her in imme-diately. The doctor on call who lived around the corner from the clinic was going to meet us there. We, on the other hand, lived eleven miles away and, with the storm, getting there was not going to be easy. But you knew this right?

Charlie went out to warm up the car while I bundled Emily Jane and got her to the car.

As we started leaving our driveway, Charlie got the car stuck in the snow. He tried to rock the car to see if he could get it out, but the car fishtailed to the side and the back end of the car had gone off the path of our driveway. We could not get the car out no matter what we did. The more we tried, the closer we got to the edge of the drop a few feet away.

I made a 911 phone call and the local Police Chief came and drove us to the clinic. He stayed with us as the doctor tended to our daughter. When we were done at the clinic, he was willing to bring us home. This made me happy as I had not thought to bring along any "snow-shoes!" I was very thankful this officer opted to wait for us.

My daughter was spiking a temperature of 105 de-grees. She had a rash that the doctor identified as the measles. I started to panic inside when I heard his words. I feared the high temperature might damage her ears af-fecting her hearing. This was not a pleasant thought, and I began reflecting on my own hearing impairment caused by a similar problem when I was just about the age she was now. The doctor gave her a shot, and gave me instructions on what to do, and what to look for while I dressed Emily Jane and we started for home.

It seemed to take forever to get home. The unclean roads made driving difficult. The Police Chief was a real trooper. He kept calm and focused. He knew his roads, and he got us home safely. Emily Jane slept in our bed with us that night, so I could watch her more closely. Like children do, she did get better and was feeling herself again in just a few days. I was relieved.

Several months more have gone by now and the winter season was ending. Warmer weather was peeking around the corner waiting to jump out and welcome us to spring. I had never been to the area before and since we had moved in the latter part of the fall season, I did not know what kind of slide show nature would present to me.

As the snow melted around us and the buds began to show up on the trees, evidence was appearing to let me know winter was done and gone for now. The melting snow brought "water falls" over the rocky cliffs on the side of the roads. The minerals from the rocks would change the frozen waters to different colors. These were pretty. I had never seen anything like this before.

Further down the road at a nearby farm, there was a very large pond. When fishing season started, I remember seeing a canoe gliding over the water of this pond. The angler had draped his pole over the side of the canoe and into the water. It was such a peaceful scene. I could imagine that Norman Rockwell would want to paint something like this. I then imagined what his painting would look like on the cover of the Saturday Evening Post magazine.

Several weeks later on this very spot are thousands and thousands and, let me say it again, thousands of dandelions embracing the sun. The angler obviously not a local resident was fishing on a flooded pasture! Now that the water had drained beneath the soil, cows were grazing there. This was a memory worth keeping locked in the files in my mind!

Back at the A-frame, the green grass was starting to sprout around us. Emily was enjoying her newfound treasures. We both basked in the refreshing mountain air, which was a lot cleaner to breathe compared to the city air we left behind at the house at the bottom of the school hill. Having fewer cars on the road made a noticeable difference in the quality of air we were breathing.

The owners of the chalet had not done a lot of creative landscaping around our place. It was plain, and lacked the colorful surroundings I grew up seeing. At least, this is what I thought when spring began. As we spent more time outside, we looked harder at what was around us, and we did manage to see more of the colors we had been missing.

There were plenty of trees, and their leaves displayed the many different shades of greens we could see. The trees would also adorn themselves with all types of living creatures. Brown and gray squirrels and nests of brown, black, yellow, red and orange birds lived among the many different types insects. These brought out all the colors that had been hiding from us. The landscape was coming alive. It was not as dull as I had first thought it to be.

We did not have many neighbors on our secluded street. Even though other chalets had been built on the street, those who lived in them kept their distance. It was so quiet that you hardly knew if the neighbors were coming or going.

I did not mind the silence. Without the hustle and bustle of city life around us, the silence allowed me to hear sounds I had never heard before. When I couldn't figure out a new sound I was hearing, Charlie would identify the sound for me. Sounds like the wind blowing through the trees or, when the windows were open in the chalet, the squirrels chattering as they scurried about here and there. I could also hear the sounds of the brook waters as they went passing by.

Occasionally, gunshots rang out letting us know hunters were nearby. We did not venture out too deeply in the woods as I was afraid the hunters would think we were deer if they heard our movements. I was more afraid that they would be shooting our way before I even had a chance to know they were in the area. I would have wanted to let them know that we were humans and not some kind of animal that they may have wanted to shoot. This would not have been good for my emotional state!

We had seen a few hunters with rifles draped across the front of their chest during the winter hunting season.

They always appeared ready to fire at their target when given a chance. On the way to or from taking Emily Jane to her sitter, I often saw trucks parked in the brush at the side of the road, and hunters would be peering out their windows waiting for deer. At times, I would see them kneeling and stooped low to the ground as they were aiming at deer. Shockingly, these hunters were only just a few feet away from the doors of their vehicles. I thought this was horrible. This did not feel like hunting should feel. To me, it looked like outright murder!

After dropping my daughter off at the daycare one day, I spotted hunters in the same spot on the side of the road where they had been favoring since the hunting season started. I will admit I was feeling a little impulsive at this moment, and I took action to stop them from having any success at killing a deer. I blasted the horn of my car until the deer looked up, sensed danger and ran off. While laying on the horn, I was yelling outside my opened window, "RUN BAMBI, RUN!" You might say that this was a very crazy thing to do. I do not suggest others do the same! It could have been life threatening if any of these hunters felt the need to retaliate and shoot me for my messing up their chances of getting a prize. The looks on their faces told me that I was facing a death sentence of my own should I dare repeat this "save the deer" stunt again!

Outside of hunting, skiing, going to the bars or grabbing a bite to eat at a local restaurant, there were not a whole lot of other entertainment options especially when spring came around. The townspeople rolled up their sidewalks at 6:30 sharp each night. There were no movie theaters, bowling alleys or shopping malls. There were a few gifts shops and ski shops that line the road going into the next town, but outside of a grocery store, these other shops closed early too. After supper, we went for walks along the brook that ran by our house. I never thought I would get such a thrill from hearing stones hit the water as they landed after we threw them. Plop! Plop! Plop! (This is what you heard if you threw more than one rock at a time into the brook). This kind of entertainment was fun and free! You didn't have to stand in line to buy a ticket and there were no time limits on how long you could stay. Plop! Plop! Plop! Is everybody having fun?

With most of the winter people in the area leaving as the snow was disappearing, Charlie and I were not able to meet many new people, and, therefore, we did not have many friends. People remaining behind when the ski resort closed their doors for the seasons were local residents or out of state folks like us who were searching for an easier, healthier way of life. Our kinds of people were labeled "flatlanders" or, more rudely, "local wannabes!" There was a definite class distinction among those who remained.

I never understood why people had to have classes and different types of elevations in the human race. We should have all been just people. After all, we all had the same basic needs. All of us needed clothes to wear, food to eat and shelter to protect us from the elements, wild animals, or other people. Ah, it was the evil root of money, power and class distinction.

At times, I felt like I was reliving my home life all over again. People could be controlling and abusive or they bullied others to make themselves feel better. I was beginning to understand that, perhaps, this was the way it was in everyday life. It was a harsh reality and not as loving as I thought life should be.

With the warmer weather and nicer days staying around, being outside more often made Charlie want to have a puppy again! He wanted Emily Jane to have a puppy. Everyone wanted a puppy except me! I kept trying to put a wedge in the idea. Charlie felt that I did not love him (here we go again), because I didn't let them get a dog.

I tried to reason with him that we did not have room for a puppy, never mind a growing puppy. I tried to reason with him that raising a puppy, like anything else, required responsibility on someone's part. (I am sure this was a concept he was not familiar with.) He just did not get the sense of any of my reasons for being against having a flea- catching, tongue-drooling, tail-wagging puppy!

I had come to learn that when Charlie set his mind on getting something, he did not stop lobbying for this yearning until he got what he wanted. His pleads were taxing on my nerves. He hounded me daily until I gave in and said, "Yes!" Less than twenty-four hours later, our new puppy was wagging her tail and loving the attention shown to her by her new owners, Charlie and Emily Jane!

The puppy and Emily Jane did everything together. Emily Jane was the apple of the puppy's eye and sole benefactress of the puppy's protection and affection. I will admit that, in just a short time, the puppy was growing on me and I was beginning to enjoy her. I liked the extra security a dog provided when we took our daily walks. Having the dog with us when we went on our walks was like having extra ears:. hearing ears, that is. The puppy always seemed to get excited when she heard a noise or picked up a scent of something moving around us. She was a good protector.

Like most puppies do as time went by, she, too, grew into a full-size dog. She was also quick to make friends with the other dogs that lived in the neighborhood. Months later, she surprised us with a litter of eight puppies, all of which looked just like her. Charlie and Emily Jane were over the moon about these additions to our household. They were enjoying every minute they were spending with this canine family.

For me, this dog and her puppies meant more work. I was the one who fed them. I was the one who took them outside to play when I came home from work. I was the one who cleaned up any messes they may have left behind during the day when we were away. It was always me, me, me!

If Charlie had his way, we would have kept all the puppies. Instead, I had to put my foot down and demand that he put an ad in the local paper advertising for free puppies. Many people responded and were smiling when they left our home with a puppy snuggled in their arms.

When we got down to one last puppy, the "how can you be so mean" looks started generating poison darts. These darts were ready to shoot my way should I dare let the last puppy leave our home! Guilt trips and continued reminders of how cruel I was behaving forced me to allow the last puppy to stay. We now had two dogs!

There were many times during this relocation experience that I felt a deep void and a sharp loneliness. I hated not having the support of my family, and I wished that my siblings would reach out to me or, at least, would try to open the door to communication. We had moved to the A-frame chalet in November, and, by the end of May the following year, contact with my family had been non-existent. I was surprised when speaking to my siblings thirty plus years later that they felt anger over my leaving abruptly, and these siblings were still harboring an intense amount of resentment. (How dare me for trying to have a start fresh and protect my child from the sick world I grew up in). It was hard for me to swallow the fact that none of them, except Louisa, who had done the same for her children, could even comprehend the decision I had made. Even though my brothers had moved out of state, they were still a part of the ongoing dysfunction, and this deeply saddened me when reuniting with the family decades later. Meanwhile, for the time being, life was continuing at the chalet filled with its own challenges and drama!

By the end of April, my work at the ski resort was ending and request for musicians to play at the lodges had stopped, too. We were not able to find new employment when our jobs ended. When the mountain closed its doors for the season, the area towns became like the ghost towns seen in the old west. There were very few options open for us to find work especially considering our transportation and childcare obstacles.

That stabbing feeling was hitting my stomach again. I began to worry about our bills and the lack of money to pay them. I can't imagine how I maintained a sense of function and calmness while having such an astronomical stress level. So, since we were not going to be able to support the A-frame chalet anymore, we needed to seek a less expensive place to live. This meant we would be moving again. By this time though, I knew the routine. I needed to pack! Ugh! I did not like this!

# CHAPTER TEN
## The Tent and Mini "RV"

*L*ess than a year after my great escape, I was in over my head trying to deal with my surmounting problems. Most of these problems stemmed around my life with Charlie. Currently, I needed to focus on our growing dilemma (soon to be homeless, with almost zero dollars in my pocket). I couldn't understand why I was making so many bad decisions. What had I been doing wrong? I was still feeling as if I was trapped in some kind of time-warp and was back reliving my childhood all over again. The fear, stomach wrenching pains and emotions were staring me in the face. Flashbacks were clouding my ability to think and think clearly. My needing to process events of my childhood to find answers for why I continued to make wrong decisions and then having to endure the resulting consequences of my bad decisions would have to take a back seat at this time. I needed to pack!

I don't want to paint a picture that misleads people to believe that I was "as white as snow." When it came to my relationship with Charlie, I, too, shared part of the blame for the problems we faced. I did not want to believe that Charlie was using me. I did not want to believe that Charlie was not a responsible person. I did not want to believe that Charlie did not love me. And, clearly, I did not want to face the fact that I had made mistakes. I was trying hard to make something work just because I wanted it to, and I didn't want to accept the fact that I was in a sinking ship. It was now clear to me that the smoke from the marijuana joints had fogged up my brain, and I had not been in my right frame of mind when I allowed Charlie to move in with me.

When Charlie originally moved in with me, he did not help with household expenses or chores. When I tried to address this issue with him, and requested that he pay half of the rent and essentials, I can still remember his response. "You would have to pay for everything if I was not here! After all, we are not married!" In other words, if I insisted that he pay half of the bills, he would just leave and find someone else to live with.

It was clear-cut. There were no secrets about how he felt or what he would do. Yet, even after knowing his answer and I could see that he would not help me around the house, I still had gotten myself pregnant. I should have evaluated my situation a little better. Although I "opted to have the baby," I should have presented Charlie with a list of my own ultimatums and demands I had for him. If he did not comply, I should have asked him to leave! I really had gone down a hard road.

From the very start of our relationship, there were many times Charlie would verbally abuse me and put me down. His words crushed and tormented my soul. Charlie really had the ability to be quite cunning. He knew how to play into my weak emotions, and he knew how to bully me. I could never seem to see how I would deserve anything better. I felt as if I would not find any other man to love me, and Charlie consistently let me know I would not get anyone else to love me either. I did, however, not always take this emotional battering quietly and sometimes I responded with my own fits of anger. It seemed pointless to voice my opinion though as Charlie did not listen when I spoke. There were times he actually yelled at me for voicing my thoughts and would say, "What have I told you about thinking?" I swallowed the words my mind was screaming to say and internalized my sorrows. When alone, I would shed many angry tears as I tried to figure out strategies to help free myself from the mess I had put myself in. I wanted a different life for my daughter. I wanted peace and honesty and my bills paid.

I regretted letting Charlie move in with me. I regretted the leverage that I had given him over my life. I resented his selfishness and his endless wants and demands on my time, and on the money that we didn't ever seem to have. Daily life with him was infused with infinite stress. Every day there would be a new list of his "must haves." It was taking an emotional toll on me. This was evident by my depression and low self-esteem. These generated emotions were reminders that I had taken a wrong path. Evidence of this fact was blinking before my eyes like a neon sign

(On, the past - Off, the present. On, the past - Off, the present). Still, I needed to overcome these feelings and keep it together all the while trying to find reasons for why I made such bad choices. Did I really know any other way? This is not how I wanted to continue living my life. I needed to work on making positive changes. However, life right now was not about me, and how degraded I felt. It was about Emily Jane and our needing to find another place to live.

Packing was going to be easier than I thought it would be. Almost everything we owned went into a box and was sealed with packing tape. Black markers scribbled notes on the brown cardboard boxes identifying the items being stored in the stomachs of each box. We were going to know exactly what was in each box at some point in the future when we would get to open them. For now, these boxes were going to be stored.

We were moving to a campground. That should have simplified things a bit. With both of us out of work and having limited funds, Charlie decided and led me to believe that the perfect solution to our situation was camping for the summer. He felt we could save money this way and have the necessary funds to get our next place in the fall. He thought this was a "wonderful idea!" I went along with his plan. At this time, I was not coming up with any bright ideas of my own.

After we had the tent set up, Charlie took Emily Jane to the play area below our campsite to let her start enjoying the "great outdoors." With the two of them gone for a little while, I took this free time to organize the inside of the tent.

Emily Jane's portable crib was set in one corner of the tent with our bed as close to hers as I could get it. It was important for me to be able to feel my daughter during the nighttime to ensure that she was warm, still safe in her crib and hadn't been carried away by any of the wild animals roaming about the campground while we slept.

A trunk that held extra clothing and bedding was placed at the foot of our bed. A table was set by the side as you entered the tent and held a lamp which would light up the inside of the tent after it was dark. I also made a bed for the dogs by the door of the tent.

Out on the picnic table, I had started preparing dinner in my electric frying pan. The pan's cover protected the food cooking inside. There were strong rules governing the removal of this cover. The cover could only be lifted, to stir the food or to check and see if it was burning! No other reasons for taking the lid off the pan would be acceptable. I did not want any bugs becoming part of my meals should they get trapped inside when I was placing the cover back on the pan. I did not need the extra calories, thank you!

As we sat at our picnic table eating our meal, I looked around our campsite and beyond at all the greens and views there were for me to take in. I was actually enjoying the change in scenery. There were no tall buildings obstructing the view of the sky. There were no run down houses where people were too poor to enjoy life. Just tall trees and a heaven full of sky above me. The only homes I could see here were the nests in the trees that looked like they had been there for some time. Large black birds were still seeking refuge in these nests wallpapered with old brown leaves. Observing sights like these left me forgetting my immediate woes and I began finding a glimpse of peace with our current situation.

Still though, I was not a happy-go-lucky camp girl. In fact, I really hated camping out in the open air. I did not like the lack of indoor plumbing, the uninvited insects that lined up outside the tent door for their chance to invade the tent, and I did not like my inability to clean the campsite to my expectations. The few peaceful moments I had just flew out of my mind's windows! I was drowning in my sorrows, again! I had to give myself a major pep talk!

Taking a very deep breath, I weighed out the pros and cons before me around outdoor living. After minutes of soul searching, I realized that getting through the various abuses and years of disappointments had had their benefits. The "boot camp" training I had received in my earlier years at home prepared me to survive just about anything that would come my way in the future. I repeatedly chanted "I can do it" until I convinced myself I could. At least, I would pretend that I could. Eventually I knew I would be able to "shake off" this experience, too. I was a survivor—YES!

It is simply amazing to learn how quickly the mosquitoes appear once the sun had gone to bed for the night.

Just like clockwork, they were surrounding us and coming at us at all angles possible. We headed to the safety
of our tent.

Charlie and Emily Jane did not move fast enough for
me and I would scream for everyone to "hurry!" I would
wildly be swinging my arms and slapping the various
parts of my body while trying to defend myself against
these flying warriors. Screaming would be part of my
defense. However, I screamed with my mouth closed! I
wasn't in the mood for any dessert at this time. No lagging was allowed! We did not need to do a lot of thinking
on the way to the inside of the tent. It was a simple task.
Just a quick dash to and a tumble into the tent would be
sufficient! But, HURRY!

Once the tent's window flaps and door were zipped,
I was able to calm myself down some. I would then get
Emily Jane ready for bed and read to her. Reading was
soothing. Shortly after reading bedtime stories, the shell
shock wore off and we would all be sound asleep!

In the morning, I was surprised at how restful my
sleep had been. It made me think about a few words I
remembered from the movie, "Heidi." At the end of this
movie, Heidi proclaims that "the healthy mountain air"
had made her friend well. I guess there could be some
truth to what she said. A slap to my arm killing something feasting on my blood brought me quickly back to
reality. I was not Heidi, I was not in the movie and I was
not living in the Swiss Alps!

Charlie and Emily Jane were still asleep as I quietly

unzipped the screen to the door and peeked out. Down the hill by the playground were a couple of deer. This was a welcomed sight to my still sleepy eyes. The deer were just there and were not bothering anyone. They were beautiful. I remember the white tail and spots on a young doe. I began thinking to myself that this was not a bad way to start the morning.

My mind again went back in time. This time, I thought about the hunters on the side of the road trying to shoot deer. I did not mind when people hunted for food to nourish their bodies, but I will never understand hunting just for the thrill of being able to say you "bagged" a deer. It did not make any sense to me. Suddenly, I began realizing that "nature" was calling me and I would have to continue this silent discussion I was having in my head a little while later. Right now, I needed to visit the restrooms, which were a distance away from the tent.

Then, without giving it a second thought, I let the dogs out. Before I knew it, the deer were gone, the dogs were gone, and the campground folks were waking up because the dogs were barking! I wanted the clouds to part and have God strike me dead. My life just never seems to get better. I never understood what I kept doing wrong. Why was living my life so difficult? Nothing in my life seemed normal. Then ,I started thinking again and came up with possible answers. Maybe this was your normal everyday life. Maybe my perspective on life was all wrong? It was all starting to make sense to me.

The tent was just a temporary living arrangement for

us when we began living at the campground. Shortly after moving here, Charlie's nephew Patrick kindly blessed us and towed our little 17-foot trailer with his van from where it had been parked before we moved to the A-frame chalet. That night while Patrick and Charlie visited and caught up on news, I did not care how many beers they drank. I was on cloud nine.

Our camp trailer had everything we needed. First and most importantly, this camp trailer had metal walls. It was higher off the ground and had a door that locked. There was a kitchen table with benches to eat our meals on inside! There was a cook stove, a tiny kitchen sink where I could bathe Emily Jane and do my dishes. There was closet space, a furnace and beds. We also had a bathroom with a shower. For now, it could not get any better than this. Pleassseee let nothing spoil this mood! I was in "hog heaven!"

Accepting that the physical items I needed to endure my current lifestyle were crammed in this 17-foot trailer, I began to realize I did not need anything else. It started feeling as if a pair of scissors was cutting the noose around my neck and relieved some of the tensions I was fighting with. Things were starting to look better to me. Maybe this was the good life after all!

What I did not need in the camp trailer were the two dogs taking up my already tight floor space. The dogs stayed outside until bedtime. On days when it was raining, I did let them stay dry with us inside. This was a great sacrifice on my part.

It did not take me long to adjust to the new routine. I realized things were not as bad as I made them out to be. I was getting the knack of cooking on an outdoor grill. I loved overcooking the hot dogs until they were burning on the outside. I loved the smell of the wood burning under the grill that held our veggies and the meat that I was cooking. I loved even more how the smoke would keep the bugs at bay and allowed me to get through the cooking part of our meal without too many problems.

The problems I still needed to work out were, one, my needing to scream because of the bugs and, two, my needing to scream again and again! Otherwise, I was finding out that my situation was not as gloomy as I had painted it to be. It was beginning to feel doable.

Shortly after we moved to the campground, the ski resort hired me for the summer working the front desk at one of the main lodges on the premises. Around this time, Charlie and I had met someone who worked at a daycare center, which we passed by on the way to my work as we traveled over the mountain.

Soon after, we registered our daughter at this daycare so she could be around other children. With the daycare enrollments increasing, Charlie was able to obtain a part time position at the facility. This allowed Emily Jane to attend the daycare at no cost on the days Charlie was working.

This was going to work out well for all of us. I was at peace knowing Emily Jane was properly cared for while I was working. Charlie had something to do and it generated funds. Emily Jane was meeting and bonding with other children. Finding this daycare center was a real blessing. This helped to make the tight living quarters easier to endure.

Back at the campground, we went to bed after the sun had set for the day. The nights passed by quickly. It seemed that not long after we went to bed, the sun was rising letting us know it was morning. A new day was beginning.

Dressing and feeding Emily Jane was easy. With her ready, Charlie would then watch her so I could go to the stalls to take my showers. After this, Charlie took his turn and we then gathered what we needed for the day and headed for the mountain.

After dropping me off at work, Charlie and Emily Jane would go to the daycare center. After work, they would pick me up and we would then tend to other needs we might have had before returning to the campground.

When we got back to the camp trailer, it seemed my work was never ending. After leaving the car, my second full-time position would begin. I had a list of things I had to do before I could sit down and rest for a minute or two. There were suppers to make, the dogs still needed to go for their walks, Emily Jane needed her baths and there were still books to read before we got to the best part of the nighttime routine: opening the little curtains above our head and watching for deer.

Emily Jane was easy to please. She had a great love for books. Any idle time I had, she would jump in my lap with an armload of books for me to read: "Bambi," "Lyle the Crocodile," and "Good Night Moon," were just a few of the books I read daily for her young ears to enjoy. After reading these books, we then read one or two other books we had obtained from the library or borrowed from the daycare center.

Keeping Charlie happy was another full time job. He always wanted more. His list and things to do was unending. He was never content with just staying home. On our days off, instead of sleeping in and relaxing, Charlie headed the family down the road to a larger town about twenty-five miles away.

While there, Charlie would visit the local music store to obtain any guitar strings, tapes or other musical items he needed. Afterwards, we would go to the fast food joints and get a bite to eat. This was a real treat for us. Emily Jane looked forward to the little toys that came with her meals. After eating our meals, we headed to the nearest shopping center to get supplies.

As a family, we enjoyed our daily walks to the brook. On extra warm days, Charles took Emily Jane with him into the deeper part of the brook. He let her kick her feet in the water as the waters were cooling their bodies. I did not go in the water. Having a fear of water, I opted to sit on the rocks at the edge of the water and swat and bat at anything that dared to come my way.

You would never believe how many bugs and flying things loved water, too! Who needed a gym out here? I certainly did not need one. I had all the exercise I needed each day just from trying to get out of the way of the bugs and the creepy things around me. I was doing arm swings, jumping exercises and, on occasion, running sprints were added to my workout routine. These exercises kept me in tiptop shape and out of the pathway of bugs!

However, if I was an entomologist, I could have written a book! There were hundreds of different species exposing themselves right before my very eyes. If our stay at the campground had lasted any longer than the five months we were there, we would have seen some of these bugs on the endangered species list. I am sure of this fact!

After weeks of doing my nightly exercises, I was surprised at the fact that I was still alive and walking. You would have thought with all the bugs sipping at my blood from the straws hanging from their mouths that in just a short period of time, they would have depleted my blood supply and I would have withered down to nothing. I had visions of people finding my lifeless body by the river. Some would have been wondering after finding me and seeing me so "white" if I was human or something else that had not been discovered and identified before. Thanks to the year supply of bug spray we had purchased, this never did happen.

With all of us keeping busy, the spring and summer months passed by quickly. Soon the cooler weather would be coming our way. The campground would soon be closing. We needed to find a permanent place to live before the snow began to fly around us.

We learned about a three-bedroom trailer that was

for sale. It was in great condition, partially furnished and the owners were willing to move it where we would live in it. We met with the realtor. After signing the papers to purchase the trailer, the former owners towed the trailer to our site. This time, Charlie, Emily Jane, the two dogs and I would be moving to the other side of the mountain where I was working.

However, before taking this next giant step, there was one more thing we had to do. Charlie and I still had some unfinished business to take care of. We had to sell the camp trailer. I never wanted to live in it again! After having lived five months in this camp trailer with concert speakers, music equipment, two dogs, Emily Jane and Charlie, I never wanted to see the camp trailer or the campground again! In just a short time, we happily found a buyer and sold our camp trailer.

We handed the new owners the keys and sent them on their way with our blessings.

# CHAPTER ELEVEN
## The Three-Bedroom Modular

*I*t was cold and damp outside, but my heart was warm inside and I was filled with hope and prospect. I was ready to move into the three-bedroom trailer we had just purchased. Two things happened after we set foot in the trailer. The first thing that happened is that during the night it snowed. The second thing was in the form of a layoff notice on my desk the next day at work. Unbelievable!

That gut wrenching feeling was gnawing at my stomach again. It felt like I had just jumped out of an airplane without a parachute. When I came crashing down, I splattered my brains all over the earth. Again and again, nothing was smooth sailing for me.

Negative thoughts were being tossed around in my mind and I felt as if I were a ship amidst stormy weather in the open sea. There was no rhyme or rhythm to these thoughts; they were overwhelming me and I felt as if I was drowning. I wondered if I was ever going to make a good decision in my lifetime. It seemed like I was always playing the childhood game of 'Red Rover.' In this game, if you were caught moving when the "light" was red, you were sent back to the starting line and had to begin your trek all over again. You were only allowed to move on a "green" light. I think I needed to replace the "green" light bulb. It must have blown a fuse a long time ago. It seemed like I was never going to make it to the winner's circle.

Despite hitting a financial snag within the first twenty-four hours of our move into the trailer, this move had been the easiest of all our moves so far. All of our boxes were already packed and had been marked. Retrieving them from storage and bringing them home was all we had to do. Packing was becoming as simple to me as making an apple pie was to my grandmother. The hard work of dismantling a home had already been done. Unpacking went smoothly and did not seem as stressful as I had this routine down to a science!

Emily Jane had her own bedroom again. Our bathroom had a shower and a tub! Charlie and I took the largest of the three bedrooms. We made the last bedroom a storage area. Eventually, you guessed it, it became Charlie's music room. The kitchen was clean. Everything was falling into place and this was making me very happy!

The dogs were happy, too. After living in a camp trailer, they loved the extra room. The dogs had more space than even they knew what to do with. These dogs now had all the outdoor space they wanted! Although, contrary to some people's opinion, my heart was not made of stone and I did let the dogs come inside at night and on colder days. If they barked, they came in right away! I did not want their barking to irritate our new neighbors. We did not have many neighbors, but I wanted to keep the ones we had on pleasant terms. We lived in a quiet area and any noise tended to echo and travel a great distance so there would be limits to the amount of barking they would be allowed to do. NONE!

The dogs liked their new surroundings. In fact, after a couple of weeks, they felt brave enough to do some exploring around the home without us, and did not always want to wait for our daily walks. Mommy dog along with her puppy dog decided to venture out on their own several times. Once they came home with a leg off a deer that had been hanging from a tree of a camp nearby hidden by clumps of trees in the deeper part of the woods. Our dogs had taken part of someone's trophy! Not good! If caught, the dogs would be guilty as charged as deer hair was shredded and shaken all around the yard and had polluted the freshly fallen snow. This was one of the first indications I began to notice of their erratic change in behavior.

I reasoned long and hard with Charlie about this situation. He needed to find the dogs a new home, NOW! He did not like this idea, but this time I did not back down until I won out. This made Charlie and Emily Jane quite upset with me but I did not care. I was afraid that the dogs would want to "eat" our little Emily Jane now that they had extended their taste buds beyond the beef flavor of a can of "Alpo." Sorry folks, I was not taking any chances.

Life continued despite the fact that the dogs had moved on to new homes at a farm nearby. Charlie was still working at the daycare center and I was volunteering on a regular basis there myself. I enjoyed reading and telling stories. I loved engaging the children in doing their arts and crafts. I loved watching the children go out the door at night, get into their cars with their mommy and daddy and drive away. This was the best part of the day. Now, we could leave ourselves and head for home.

Things at home were tense. My relationship with Charlie had not grown any stronger. We continued to have mounting financial problems. Our having moved deeper into the countryside was not going to help make it easier for us either. Other than a small country store, there was not much in the area in the way of options for employment or economy. Yet, I was determined to make our family a success for my daughter's sake and I kept trying to do all I could and continued to work on making our home life more peaceful. Was I becoming delusional?

Charlie imagined ways he could help, but it was hard to make his ideas a reality in this desolate area. Adding to all this, Charlie was feeling the effects of the isolation. He missed having the ability to party and socialize with others. He missed the city life. He was missing the friends he left behind.

Even though I tried to be understanding about his needs, I was not going to leave Emily Jane with a babysitter in the middle of "nowhere land" or go back to smoking marijuana. Charlie would have to make the best of his situation. He continued to focus his concerns on his music.

In the meantime, Emily Jane was growing and thriving. She was almost two years old and had the maturity of a forty-year old person! When we had family discussions, she was not shy about voicing her thoughts. She was observant and very, very smart for her age. When reading her stories, you couldn't take any short cuts. No, No, she would let us know if we passed over a word or skipped a page. Kids! What would we do without them?

Deer were common visitors to our property so the story of "Bambi", which I read several times a day, became part of our daily routine. It was Emily Jane's favorite story. However, I did not like violence and Emily Jane was such a sensitive girl even at two that when I read her this story, I always left out the part where the hunters kill Bambi's mother. My innocent little girl had no clue that this was ever part of the book even after having heard the story at least a thousand times!

Once during the following summer, Charlie wanted to take Emily Jane to an outdoor theater. At this particular time, they were actually showing the movie "Bambi." I thought this was a great idea. I loved the fact that she could see an animated version of the story. I just knew she was going to love seeing her friends in "action." WRONG! WRONG! DOUBLE WRONG!

While we were peacefully sitting in the car watching the movie, I somehow had forgotten the part where

Bambi's mother dies and I was NOT prepared when this part came up on the screen. I had left this part of the story out for so long that I had forgotten it was part of the true version of the story. Emily Jane became hysterical and was becoming a disturbance to those around us. She could not be comforted and carried on long after we got home. She was also angry at me for not telling her the truth about Bambi's mother. She was angry that I had made her see Bambi's mother get shot and die! After Emily Jane had fallen asleep that night, I threw the "Bambi" book in the trash. Never to be read again! This was "The End" of this story!

As much as Emily Jane loved to be read to, she also had an ear for music. She had a drum of her own. She felt good about her ability to play and enjoyed creating her own music. On one of our outings to the "big city," Charlie had purchased a "real" set of drumsticks for Emily Jane when he was at the music store. She used these to explore all the different sounds in the trailer. She hit everything around her to see what sound it would make: the walls, pots and pans, the tables, everything.

Hitting or rather smacking her father on the head to see what type of sound he would make was not a good idea! Let's just say Charlie did make "noise" and plenty of it. His "noise" was loud and his tone rang out in several different octaves of the musical scale! I am sure it was not the type of music Emily Jane was anticipating. His screams sent little Emily Jane running into her bedroom to hide. At this time, Charlie was running around the trailer screaming like a mad man! When he brought his screaming down a notch, he took Emily Jane's drumsticks, proceeded to open the trailer door and heaved them as hard and far as he could into the winter snow! These drumsticks remained out of sight until the snow melted in the spring! Ouch!!

Charlie was a die-hard television viewer. Unlike most people, the TV guide was his "Bible." There was no cable TV in our area at this time. Although cable was available in some of the surrounding towns, it had not come our way yet.

Charlie was beside himself. He would literally spend hours trying to get the picture on the television set to come in more clearly. The rabbit ear antenna had been bent in every direction possible in search for a better picture. For Charlie, a day without television reception was like a day without sunshine for a farmer. If the weather conditions interfered with the already hard-to-get reception, he was miserable.

A few months after moving to the trailer, I found what looked like marijuana around and about the kitchen sink. My blood was rising as I was thinking that Charlie was smoking pot again! I did not say anything right away. Anyone can have a setback.

However, after seeing this marijuana around the sink for several days in a row, I started rummaging through the cabinets to find this "bag" of pot so I could throw it away. I was shocked to find that a mouse had been visiting during the nighttime and had chewed his way through a can of parsley! It was parsley I found on my counter in the morning!

I made a mental note to apologize to Charlie for assuming he was doing drugs again and in our home. I reasoned that since I had not yet accused him, he had not known what I had been thinking. Therefore, I felt I did not need to apologize. I was just going to seek out all the facts before ever blaming him for something like this again. A mousetrap on the counter the following night took care of the problem. This was just a temporary fix as other mice would eventually seek shelter in our home, too. Just when I thought my "trauma" plate was full, life threw me a curve ball and gave me something else I would have to deal with! EEEKKKK!

Soon, however, I would learn that I was not the only one on this earth that had a mouse-a-phobic problem. A few months after we moved into the three-bedroom trailer, Charlie's nephew Patrick came for a visit. He brought with him, Liz, his wife-to-be. They would be our first overnight guest in our new home since we moved away from the house at the bottom of the school hill.

We were excited as visits from any family members or friends from our hometown were few and far between. Many of these people still thought that because we were so isolated from any form of real life that we had gone back in time and "Indians" were still living in the area. They were afraid the "Indians" would attack us while they were visiting. They also thought there was a chance the bears might pounce on them and shred them to pieces if they came to our home. Patrick and Liz were the first to have the courage to venture into the "wild" to stay with us for a night!

It was nice to sit with Patrick and Liz and get undated information on what was happening back home. I had set the table with cloth linens and we all sat around enjoying the home cooked meal I had made.

Our guest wanted to turn in early as they were tired from their travels. They were also hoping to be able to get some skiing in while they were here and wanted to rest up for an early start in the morning. Shortly after eating, I made up the couch bed. This is where our brave guest would sleep for the night.

We then turned down the lights and when Emily Jane was asleep in her bed, Charlie and I went to bed ourselves. However, some unexpected minor events transpired during the night. Unfortunately because of this, a few of us were not able to get a good night's rest. A MOUSE had walked on Liz's face! Nooooo, we were not going to sleep tonight!

We all tried for hours to calm Liz. Nothing we said or did would work. She had it fixed in her mind that "calm" was not going to happen! She spent the rest of the night jumping at any noise she heard.

We had been used to hearing the furnace kick on from time to time during the night. However, for someone who was not used to the noise and just had a mouse walk on her face, the noise slightly tested her nerves. After the furnace kicked on, we would hear the soft muffled sounds that Liz would make. Patrick's voice followed these whimpers as he quietly assured Liz that everything was okay. After a few minutes, she would settle down only to freak out again when the furnace kicked back on. This cycle continued throughout the night and right on into the break of dawn. First thing in the morning, Patrick and Liz packed up their luggage and headed out the door to the nearest motel room they could find. They did not even wait to eat the country breakfast I had planned on making them. They were just gone! They never visited or stayed with us again. I might add also that we never did receive a "thank you" card from them! I had spent a lot of time making sure that the house was extra clean for them. I had even left the "light" on for them! That's gratitude for you!

It was relieving to know that spring was just around the corner. The spring season brought with it the rain. Lots and lots of rain! As the rains poured down on our trailer, the ants that had awakened from their winter siesta were seeking drier places to nest. They were choosing our house to dry off! One by one, they would come out from the furnace, go up the wall, across the paneling, through the living room and into the area of the kitchen sink. Eventually I sat on a bar stool in front of the furnace, with my fly swatter in hand, and I would kill every ant that attempted to make his way out of the furnace and into my home. It wasn't happening. Who needed a can of RAID when my aim was GREAT! Whacking these little daring black ants caused the metal casing around the furnace to rattle sending out sounds that echoed throughout the trailer.

After a while, the rumbling noise from the hollow furnace and my continuing need to smack these ants drove Charlie completely NUTS! Finally, he was going to do something about it! You think? It took one hundred and twenty dead ants before he took action! I am glad they were not poisonous. Anyway, he took a little time and searched to find where these ants had marked as their entry way into our home and he plugged the little hole.

With his nerves a little frazzled after a week of smacking the fly swatter on the echoing furnace, Charlie took us to a motel for a retreat. As I looked up on the headboard of the bed when laying down, I noticed four very large carpenter ants that were a thousand times larger than the ants at our home and I felt this great need to SCREAM! Therefore, I did just that—a lot of screaming! Tonight, Charlie could have two six-pack of beer if he wanted to. He earned them!

That year, the ants had the vote of everyone around us for winning the "Pest of the Year Award!" They were everywhere! We had such a rainy spring that year and, with the outdoors being so wet, these ants had been driven out of their underground homes and sought alternative shelter. It did not matter to me when I was told why we had such an epidemic of ants in our area. I still did not like it. Screaming would be part of my being able to vent my discontentment over the situation before me. End of story!

Still not having found employment, I tried to find ways to keep myself busy. Emily Jane was riding her little tricycle in the yard and I did some much needed yard work when she was outside. Lo and behold, you would not believe, we found the DRUMSTICKS! Can you believe it? I put them in the trash. I was not going to take a chance that Emily Jane would want to see what type of sound my head would make. Putting them in the trash was good! Anyway, with the air so fresh and exhilarating and the fact that I needed to work off some of my own bottled energy, I decided that I would start "running" again. Let those positive endorphins flow! I figured it would keep me out of the trailer and away from the ants. While I was running, perhaps, I could block them out of my mind. This felt like a very therapeutic idea and I was anxious to put this plan into action. I really needed an outlet! By now, with all I had been through in my lifetime, you would have thought my nerves would be numb. Nope, no, no, and no, they were still very much alive!

Charlie stood on the side of the road with Emily Jane by his side. My plan was to run for about fifteen minutes until I could build up my stamina and then I would run for longer periods of time. With my headphones on my head, music pumping into my ears, sneakers tied and secured on my feet, I took off down the road. When I got to the curved part of the road just a little way up the street, I noticed a "black" spot ahead of me.

As I ran, I kept my eye on this slow moving "black" spot. However, this "spot" was getting bigger as I was getting closer to it. I suddenly realized that this "black" spot was a "BEAR CUB!" I turned, quickened my pace and high-tailed it back toward the trailer before I could be "eaten" by any "MOMMA BEAR" that might be following close behind her cub! Maybe, I was going to be "pounced on and shredded to pieces" after all! Maybe the fear our family and friends' fear about visiting us was legitimate! I did not want to be the first to test this theory out.

Panting and almost breathless, I made my way back home in record time and was thankful to still be in one piece. Charlie was still standing on the side of the road where he had been when I left at the start of my trek. Emily Jane was still by his side. I frantically began waving my arms and motioning for them to get inside the trailer. I think my words were loud when I started telling them why as I grabbed my daughter, and these words got louder as I headed for the trailer leaving Charlie in the dust as I passed!

After we were all safe behind the inside walls of our home and the doors were locked, I calmly explained to Charlie and Emily Jane what had happened, or rather, what I saw. I also made it clear to them (as I had resolved myself to accept) that screaming was going to be something I was going to do for the rest of my life! They needed to accept this fact, too!

What I was not going to do anymore was running outdoors. This may not compare to Liz's experience with the mouse when she visited a short while back, but I think it was going to be a tie or a very, very close call.

Our three-bedroom trailer was sitting on a very large piece of property. It rested on a small hill just below the backside of the mountain I had worked at one time. Large open fields made our trailer stand out more. It looked lonely and out of place around all of nature's beautiful landscaping. It was not your typical country house. Neither was it the kind of home you pictured in your mind when you imagined yourself living in seclusion on a mountain. There were no fireplaces or chimneys or cord wood stacked somewhere on the property. It did not fit into the normal winter scenes depicted on greeting cards.

Newer chalets and lodges were going up all around us. I was used to standing out in a crowd, I was used to being different, and looking different and having people talk about me. At this time in my life, I did not let how people viewed me bother me anymore. I was in a new mind set now. Maybe I would be described by a psychiatrist as "crazy." I am not going to deny this not being a possibility. But, I don't think that "Prozac" had the power to make this go away. I was convinced that my "crazy" lifestyle and appearance was permanent!

I was a lot stronger now, and I did not care what people were thinking about me. "Welcome to my life" was all I could say in my defense. Could these people sitting in judgment of Charlie and me have done any better than we had in our situation? I would have wanted to see them try! Bring it on!

I did not mind being away from my family, I did not mind the isolation as much anymore, and I did not mind the lack of money, either. I think a delusional depression of some sort was starting and it had become a dark cloud over me. I did wonder if I had what it would take to face the challenges continuing to come my way. Would I be able to survive the unbelievable domino effect that entrapped me? Would there be any better days ahead? Only the passing of time would give me these answers. The only thing I did know for sure was that I had to keep putting one foot in front of the other for my beautiful daughter's sake. I wanted her to grow up normal—let's laugh at this one together shall we?

# CHAPTER TWELVE
## The Two Brown Houses

$A$s you would only imagine, after several months of not being able to make our trailer payments, the previous owners took their trailer back. Not having been able to find work after my job ended on the mountain and with Charlie only working part time, we had taken a very serious financial plunge.

The previous owners understood our plight and they kindly gave us some time to seek an alternative living arrangement. We took the next couple of weeks to scout the area and see what options were open to us. Thankfully, we did find affordable housing. The rent of this house would be less than the trailer payment and this would put our finances closer to within our means. It wasn't the total solution to our financial problems, but the lower rent did help some. So, less than two years, (one year and six months to be exact) after leaving the house at the bottom of the school hill, we were moving again! This would be the fourth time. Let's see. Are we having fun yet? Let me check my diary.

I was overwhelmed with a great humiliation. If I could

have gotten a dime or even a penny for every tear I had shed over this matter, I would have been very rich. Living in a small town did not help our situation. I felt the sting. Everyone in town knew why we lost our home and why we had to move again. Their stares were familiar. Stares like the ones people gave my siblings and me when we were growing up around the "secret" four-way affair.

Moving under these circumstances understandably sent my nerves spiraling downward and I dug myself deeper into the depth of despair. I did not share with Charlie how I was feeling. It would have been a waste of my words and time. When I had anything to say or had something to suggest, he would appear to be listening but his eyes looked straight ahead. He really was not hearing what I had to say. Still, I was determined to plug along and do my best to pick up the pieces again and to keep trying to make better choices while accepting that it probably would never get any better than this. My current living situation and my continuing to live with Charlie were going to be a major challenge to this test.

Emily Jane was very adaptable. I worked hard to keep it peaceful around her during the changes she, too, was experiencing. I did not want her to build towers of bad feelings about herself or her parents. I wanted to spare her from the emotions of having to live with the consequences, good or bad, because of her parents' choices and actions. I wanted to keep her the "child" she was and for her to reap a childhood full of good memories. I wanted her to stay the innocent child I saw when I interacted with her as her mother.

Connecting the two brown houses together was a little hall. In the main part of the house is where Emily Jane had her bedroom. The kitchen was a lot bigger than the one I had in the three-bedroom trailer. There was a large living room and a bathroom with a shower off the living room.

There was one other bedroom in the other part of the house. However, I did not want to be separated from Emily Jane at night. So, for the time being, Charlie and I slept in the living room on a couch that pulled out into a bed. My hearing impairment kept me looking for assurance that I would be able to hear Emily Jane if she would need me during the nighttime. I wanted to be able to reach her if need be and in case of a fire, too. Keeping close to our daughter helped me to sleep at night.

I kept busy unpacking boxes as Charlie brought them into the house. Emily Jane followed me from room to room and spent time in her new bedroom becoming acquainted with her new surroundings. Her pink dollhouse went against the corner wall. Next to the dollhouse is where her large collection of stuffed animals and other toys were stored. We lined her many books on a smaller bookshelf on another wall. The remaining wall is where her bed and bureau rested. As she connected and made friends with her new living space, I could see that Emily Jane was proud of her room and was feeling content. I was happy to note that moving had not seemed to disturb her inner peace.

Once the boxes were all in the new house, Charlie busied himself with his newfound space too. The large family room in the other part of the house would now be his newest "music" room. Immediately, he set about arranging all his equipment and then proceeded to remove one of his many guitars from the case that held it and plugged the guitar cord into the amplifier and the electric amplifier cord into the outlet on the wall and started playing! He was in his own little world and, for now, I was okay with this. I am sure he had his own "not so good" feelings about himself right now and this room would be just the right place for him to release any emotions he felt around the move and our horrid financial situation. Music would be good therapy for him.

Emily Jane and I spent much of our time learning the new "surprises" waiting for us to discover around the outside of our new home. There were deep purple violets growing alongside of the red and yellow flowering Indian paintbrushes in the stretch of grass in front of the house. I had never seen flowering paintbrushes before. I was thrilled about our discoveries and was eager to learn more.

Little pine trees had been planted along the edge of the stretch of grass nearest to the side of the road. Lining the edges closest to our dirt driveway were plants with variegated leaves sporting light purple flowers on the end of their long-extended stems. These pretty flowers were unfamiliar to me and I had never seen the likes of them before.

At the furthest end of the property, a pond collected any water that drained from the hill above it after the snow melted or when it rained. This pond was teeming with life. Wonderful! Emily Jane and I would walk around the pond with our sticks in hand. We would hit the sticks on the ground as we walked. If there were any frogs, these would hop into the pond before we could reach them.

This was okay as it was unlikely I was going to try to catch any of them! Several times, we were able to see glimpses of snakes slithering into the water. YES, we would always have a stick with us and YES, we would always hit the ground ahead of our steps to scare any creepy, hopping, slithering thing into the pond before I had a chance to step on them and have to wear out my vocal cords screaming!

A very large ash tree shaded the left side of the pond. It was here that we decided to put Emily Jane's new swing set with slide and seesaw. Emily Jane loved being on the swing. When she pumped her little legs up and down, she would swing back and forth while her blonde hair was blowing lightly in the breeze. As I stood along the side of the pond watching her, I re-membered my own moments of peace I had felt when doing the same during my childhood years at the white house on top of the hill.

Up on the hill behind the swing set was a sand pit. We took many walks up this hill looking for deer. There were huge piles of sand that mirrored the sand dunes I had seen when I had gone to the beach. A large faded-red steam shovel, old and broken down, stood out among the sand piles. It looked as if it had lost its "steam" a long time ago and just sat there resting. Kind of like an old mare out in pasture. The mare would be standing there but it did not do much of anything else.

There was a brook across the street from us. The waters were so clear that you could see the fish swimming below the top of the water. After the snow melted in the spring, the brook waters would be high. At times, we could hear the boulders hitting one another as rushing waters, passing by, would move them. The noise was loud enough for me to hear from across the street, and from inside my house. It gave me an opportunity to learn the magnificent power behind the movement of water, and I could then imagine the power behind waves of a tsunami. Indeed, a powerful display of action.

In the fall, the leaves from the trees by the brook looked like a colorful canopy gracefully hanging over the top of the water. Fallen leaves floated like little orange, red and yellow boats as they glided down the brook.

During the summer, all of us would sit in the brook below the little waterfalls created by the stone and boulders. The soothing waters running over our bodies were cool and provided us comfort from the heat.

I loved being able to hear the noises the brook made. In the summertime, I could not hear these sounds when in our house across the street like I had during the early spring months. But, as we would sit by the brook, I loved how my ears would open and take in all the lovely sounds.

The brook would "talk" to us if we listened carefully.

Further down the road at this same brook, our small town held a "fishing derby" every year for the local children. Charlie and I had taken Emily Jane in the spring when fishing season started and let her participate in the derby with the other children.

Draping her little toy fishing pole into the water with a wiggling worm on the end of the hook, Emily Jane looked so proud and was feeling like a "big girl." It was her father who put the worm on the hook. But, you probably already knew this!

The derby did not end until all the children had hooked a fish. Then after weighing and measuring all the catches, the judges awarded prizes to the winners of the various categories in the contest: the longest, the heaviest, the first catch, etc. With her father helping her, eventually Emily Jane caught her fish to have measured and weighed. I wanted to take a picture for our photo album and had Emily Jane stand by the car with the fish dangling from the end of her fishing pole. Suddenly, Emily Jane realized the fish was DEAD! She started carrying on like her dad had done when she hit him on the head with her drumstick. All the while, Emily Jane was screaming and crying that we had made her kill a fish! In her eyes, we had made her a MURDERER! I had forgotten that the brook fish were her "friends!" It was going to be another long night!

To try to distract Emily Jane from the horrible memories of killing one of her "friends," Charlie brought home a little kitten for her. Wasn't this sweet of him? The black angora kitten became her new playmate and friend. This kitten was a little different from the friends she had been playing with at the daycare center. She loved this kitten, fed her, loved her, played with her, and loved her some more. The time they spent together was priceless. No toy could have brought her as much happiness and joy as this little ball of fur.

Day after day, I would see Emily Jane pushing the kitten in her pink doll stroller up and down the driveway. There were times the kitten had been dressed in something from Emily Jane's wardrobe. The kitten would stay in the doll stroller and enjoyed the ride she was being given.

As I sat on the porch watching my daughter play, she was always holding this tiny kitten a prisoner in her arms. It did not matter what she was doing. She was always holding the kitten. When she was pushing herself on the swing or when she walked around the yard, the kitten was in her arms. This would help her later on in life when trying to multi-task while holding her "Blackberry." While Emily Jane held this kitten in the "headlock" position, the rest of the kitten's body would be dangling below Emily Jane's arms. The kitten never struggled to break free from her grip. She just hung there. I never saw a kitten respond as lovingly as this one did. The cat stayed with Emily Jane the whole time she was outside in the yard with her.

Charlie always had something more that he needed or

wanted. After all, Emily Jane just got a cat. Shouldn't he get something too? Before the winter season had begun, he had done some "wheeling and dealing" and traded something he owned for a used snowmobile. Okay?

During the winter months, he spent many hours riding to the sand pit and on the farmland beyond the sand pit. We had previously gone to the farmer's house up the road to ask permission to ride on his land. Cross-country skiers living in the area loved the trails left behind by the snowmobile. These tracks made their skiing trips more enjoyable.

In the field across the road, Charlie had made an oval track, which looked something like a small racetrack. Emily Jane and I would dress in our snowsuits and, after putting our helmets on, we would take turns driving the snowmobile. I would sit Emily Jane on the seat in front of me and would hold her when it was her turn to "drive." She loved every minute of her time on the snowmobile.

A few times during large snow storms when the main road had not yet been plowed, we took the snowmobile up to the sandpit and over the barbed wires through the farmer's fields and came in the back way to the store. The unsettled area, the peaceful woods, and the open fields made these trips enjoyable. What would generally take us only ten minutes on foot to walk to the store from our house now would take over an hour to go in through the back way on the snowmobile. We didn't care. We were warm, content and loving it!

Winter snow from our driveway was plowed to the

edges of our pond. Living below and around a mountain range, we got our fair share of snow. Added inches were piling up by the pond. This hid the pond from our view when standing on the front porch. Unless you had been to our home before the winter, you would not have known the pond was there.

Neighborhood youths would come around from time to time and would follow Charlie as they went riding on their snowmobile up and around the sand pit. The course for the trek brought these riders down our driveway, across the snow collecting on the "edge" of the property by the side of the road, and then they proceeded up the hill to the sandpit area. Fired up for the ride, these daring and young riders would leave our front porch, jump on their snowmobiles and then they would race one another down the driveway.

However, one of the teenage boys who had joined the group of riders for his first time kept to the left side of the other riders as he rode down the driveway. He did not know about the hidden pond. He increased his speed hoping to get ahead of the other riders and he drove his snowmobile up the mound of snow at the end of the driveway and right into the pond!

I had been out on the porch and had been watching as they took off and never in my life expected anything like this to happen. When helping the youngster out of the pond, I was happy to note that he had not hurt himself. He was rightfully shaken up some but not hurt. After pulling the snowmobile out of the pond with our vehicle, giving the teen some dry clothes to wear and some hot chocolate to warm his insides, we all sat there retelling the mishap and laughing our heads off. It was hard not to look at the boy sitting in the chair shell-shocked and not laugh. Relating this experience to others who came to our home would set the friends roaring all over again. I had to admit this was funny. However, I did feel bad for the teen. His father just had the snowmobile overhauled so I knew he would be in some sort of trouble with his dad when he got home.

Even with some "good" times behind us, tension was still building up between Charlie and me to the point that I decided to leave Charlie. I took Emily Jane with me. During my week away, I used this time to try to sort out the problems I was having with Charlie. I spent long hours on the telephone with Charlie planning what we could change to keep our family together. Charlie pleaded with me to come back and I was feeling that maybe this time since we had been away from each other and had our long talks that we might actually have some improvements to our relationship. I did go back. I took another chance.

Shortly after going back to the two brown houses, and with collective effort on both our parts, there was some evidence we had made slight temporary improvements. Charlie had gotten himself a position at a group home and I spent more time with Emily Jane at the daycare center. Home life was beginning to show hope of smooth sailing.

Not long after reuniting with Charlie, I discovered that I was pregnant again. Although I was concerned about the stresses it would add to our relationship, I was thrilled to be having another baby. Emily Jane was almost four years old and loved the idea of having a brother or sister.

I was enjoying my pregnancy and the new life I was carrying inside me. We spent a lot of time explaining the natural process of our developing baby with Emily Jane. We looked at pictures from books displaying the development of the baby at the different stages.

I had further explained to Emily Jane that because I would need surgery when the baby was ready to be born, the baby would not be born as shown on the pages in the book. After thinking for a few moments about my comments, Emily Jane asked "why we had to wait nine months?" Emily Jane wanted to go in the kitchen, get a knife and take the baby out NOW! I made a mental note to sleep with one eye open that night. I took the books back to the library first thing in the morning! She can learn more about the natural process of childbirth on her own when she is older and she is pregnant with her own baby!

Nine months later, we welcomed our son Ryan into our family. Like his sister, Ryan was beautiful. He was premature but healthy. He weighed less than five pounds and was twenty-three inches long. He was going to be a tall boy when he grew up.

Emily Jane was happy that her brother was finally here. Charlie was accepting the idea of having another baby in the house and making adjustments. He was over-joyed to have a son, but not too happy with the work that came with a newborn. I was healing from my C-section and was basking in the joys that came from holding, feeding and loving our baby. Even though I knew from the start of my pregnancy that I would have most of the responsibilities in caring for our son, I was still happy!

Ryan was a good baby. Emily Jane was a good sister. She was also a great mother's helper as she helped me care for her brother. She sat with Ryan and read him stories. Other times, she would entertain him with toys while I did household chores. When taking our daily walks, I would push Ryan in the stroller. Emily Jane would be pushing her doll carriage in front on me and the cat would be following close behind us. It was quite a sight to see.

The added member to our family would not be a distraction for Charlie. He still had his music room where he could go to "hide." His focus was still on his music and he was starting a new band. This band had two trumpet players, a bass guitarist, a drummer and Charlie played the lead guitar and was the lead singer. I loved hearing the trumpets and the fact that I was able to feel the music they made. On his days off from work, Charlie and his other band members practiced for hours and hours.

Just like all the other members of his family, Ryan loved music too. When he heard the band play their music, he would jump up and down to the beat of the music when he was in his jumper. This served two purposes. One, Ryan got his exercise and his little legs were getting stronger. And two, he was distracted for a little while so I could spend some quality time alone with Emily Jane.

About a year after Ryan was born, I had obtained a nighttime position at the group home that Charlie was working at. After getting the children bathed and ready for bed, I would spend a few moments reading to them before I left for work.

While I was working, Charlie watched the children until they went to bed. In the mornings, Emily Jane and Ryan would be waiting on the porch ready to greet me when I came up the driveway. Most of the time, Ryan's diapers were on backwards or falling down, and Emily Jane would be half naked. The house looked as if a cyclone had gone through it but still, I loved coming home and seeing their smiling faces. I loved being their mother.

After eating our breakfast and putting Ryan down for his nap, I would spend time with Emily Jane and do household chores. When she went down for her nap in the afternoon, I took this time to sleep myself. For a while, Charlie would tend to the children for a couple of hours after they had awakened from their naps allowing me a few extra hours of needed sleep. I truly appreciated this gesture. I would catch up on my sleep on my days off. But, I don't believe we truly ever make up any sleep we missed. Those hours would be lost and gone forever. Bye-bye!

Not long after I had started working, Charlie and I got married. He had a weak moment and felt that because we had children, we should be married. I did not want to marry Charlie but I was hoping it would be in the children's best interest, and I was hoping our getting married might improve our relationship. Ryan was almost two years old at this time and Emily Jane had just turned five years old.

I thought about this and decided I would marry Charlie. Maybe he would treat me better now that I was going to be his wife. He was probably hoping as my husband that I would treat him better, too. My advice for anyone getting married is to not think beyond what you see in front of you or what you see in the mirror. If the love and respect is not there before you get married, it is not going to be there after. Wishing is not going to make changes, people have to. This was another hard lesson for me to learn.

We did get married and I continued working the night shift. However, Charlie was growing tired of baby-sitting his children while I worked at night. Eventually he started hounding me to find a babysitter to watch Emily Jane and Ryan while I slept. His needing to do the baby-sitting was infringing on his practice time and he did not like this. I could not believe this. His focus was still on his music and not on his family.

I did not get a babysitter. This really added to the problems between Charlie and me. He took his frustrations out on me and was becoming verbally abusive (more so). I would take his abuse for a while and then I started lashing out myself. It got to a point where I felt "enough was enough." I did not want our children to grow up seeing this abuse. I did not want them to think I was the person Charlie said I was when he was shouting at me. I was not going to continue to accept his behavior. I started feeling like I was living back home all over again. So, eight months after we got married, Charlie and I separated.

I quit my job and took this time to be with my children. I wanted to help them through the rough changes they were facing and we were facing as a family. I had thought it was going to be hard on the children with their father gone but it was so peaceful and stress free in the home now that I think Emily Jane and Ryan were accepting that their father was not with us. I kept them busy and we spent our days doing picture puzzles, coloring, painting, playing with play dough and building things with the building blocks. We also played together racing some of Ryan's fifty-plus matchbox cars.

The house was clean, quiet and I liked the solitude I was experiencing during the times I spent with my children. We had a consistent routine. We ate our meals together. We listened to and danced to music. We even took time to plant a little garden. We had some carrots, onions, potatoes and lots and lots of tomatoes! Once a week we had a ritual. We dug up the plant on the edge of the rows and looked under the dirt to see the progress the vegetables were making.

Charlie went out of his way to buy Emily Jane and Ryan toys during his time away from the family. He brought these toys with him when he had visitation. Toys were not what they really wanted. They wanted quality time with their father. They would have been just as or even more content if he had read them a story or drew pictures with them. I was feeling bad for Charlie as I could see that he was not reading their hearts. He would have to learn for himself that he could not buy their love. This was not how true love worked.

Away from Charlie and beginning to feel peaceful within myself, I started to work on my own self-esteem. I also did what I could to ensure that the children had their physical and emotional needs met. I wanted Emily Jane and Ryan to be secure and know that they had a mother who would be strong and could stand on her own two feet and take control of her life.

With Charlie gone, the married couple up the street started coming around more often. They were a nice middle aged couple who always treated the children kindly. We shared many lunchtime meals together. They were fixing up their house at the time and had a very large back yard that was clean and neat. (In other words, I could leave my "stick" at home). They had a huge garden and shared many of their fresh veggies with us. And, they had lots of chickens, geese, ducks, a turkey and a peacock. These they kept in the coop in their back yard at night. During the day, these birds had free reign of the property. The children loved mingling among these birds and looking for feathers or any eggs they could find that were scattered about. Collecting these was like going on a treasure hunt.

Every day, we walked up to this house so the children could visit with the birds. At times, we would feed them or help put them in the coop for the night. When the husband and his wife went out of town, we were privileged to feed and care for the birds while they were gone. We looked forward to the times they would go somewhere so we could extend our services. Gardens and animals have a way of soothing. It brought much comfort to all of us.

When we first met this couple, we helped them do odd jobs around their property. We never took a penny for any of the work we did. I felt we were already getting more than money could buy when they shared their animals with us and I wanted to teach the children that helping a neighbor and being neighborly was not all about money. It was about showing our love for our neighbor and being able to help them in their time of need. However, they were able to accept any of the homemade treats that came out of the oven or any meals they bought for us when we had gone with them for rides in the country.

The husband was a spiritual-minded person. He spent hours sharing Bible truths with me. Even though I had read parts of the Bible at one time on my own, when he spoke about God's Word, I began to understand its message more clearly.

I thoroughly enjoyed our discussions as I truly did want a relationship with God. There was no doubt in my mind that I needed His help and direction in my life. From all that I was learning, I knew I had some changes to make. One thing for sure, I needed to sweeten my words when I spoke and more so when I was angry. I needed to be kinder to Charlie. God's Word was teaching me that I needed to have love for all my neighbors and this would include Charlie.

As I worked on my flaws, I found myself getting stronger emotionally. When I looked in the mirror, I was starting to see a better image of myself. I was all for working on becoming the real person I was inside. I began to see why I had so many problems. Granted, some of these problems stemmed from the emotional scars of my earlier years, but adding to this, I was learning that many of the problems I had were the consequences of choices I had made or because of things I did or should have done. There can be something to be said for those of us who can truly examine ourselves and have the strength to make needed changes. It felt as if I was given a boost of self-esteem that made me see the fresh start I could make that would lead me and my children onto a better road in life. It gave me a brand new beginning.

Our daily living situation became easier to deal with as I started taking some positive steps forward. My hardest trial came when I had to quit smoking. Smoking led to diseases and eventually diseases would lead to death. I wanted my children to have every opportunity at a better life than the one I had lived. I wanted to be here for them as long as possible to help, guide and direct them.

After living at the two brown houses for three years, the property owners decided that the house needed to have some serious remodeling work done on it. They opted not to renew my lease. They needed the house to be empty so they could store their tools and supplies while they worked on the different house projects throughout the summer. Then, they were going to put the house on the market for sale. So, of course, I complied with their wishes and once more, we were moving again. This time, Charlie was not around to help with the packing or anything else that had to be done when moving. It was all going to be my job! (Let's see, should I have been surprised?)

# CHAPTER THIRTEEN

## The Farm House

Finding our next place to live was easier than I thought it would be. A friend told me about a place we could rent that was just a little further into the belly of the woods. Before I knew it, the children and I had packed up, moved our things and we were unpacking in our new place. Of all the houses I had lived, I loved living at this house the best. Its history in the walls and surroundings of the property made me feel as if I had traveled back in time, maybe one hundred years or more.

The kitchen was old fashioned as you would have imagined. I would often think about some of the chores a woman who may have lived in the house then had to do. Canning the vegetables and the fruit grown on the property was one of these, for sure. I could picture the jars lined up in the cupboards. Other chores such as milking the cows, washing and ironing, mending, knitting, cleaning the home and, still yet, cooking for her family surely kept her busy. The wallpaper covering the walls and the checkerboard tile floors in the kitchen had not been replaced for a number of decades. The room was spacious.

On the wall behind the old stove was a unique feature I had never seen before. I had not seen this in movies or in any books I had read. It was a window that had been cut into the makeup of the wall.

Back in the days, this window when opened during the wintertime allowed the heat given off by the cows in the attached barn to help keep the kitchen warm or the heat from the kitchen kept the cows warm. Whatever the reason, I now understood why the farmer's wife did a lot of baking back then. The aroma from the oven helped to keep the stench from the barn in control. It also made the kitchen smell a lot nicer. There was a ledge in front of the window, where I assume is where the wife cooled any casseroles or pies she might have baked. This was all nice theoretically, but I think I still would have preferred a can of flower scented GLADE!!

The house had a large living room with a bedroom off to the side of it. A bathroom with shower was around the corner from these rooms. There was a door that led to the basement. I did not open this door nor did I have any interest in going down to see what it had to offer us. This door remained closed, by me anyway, for the whole time I lived in this house. I had enough memories from past experiences with basements, and did not want to add any new ones to my "things I needed to forget files," if there were some to be had.

However, we did share the basement space with a snake! A friend of ours had gone into the basement to change a fuse in the fuse box for me, and made this proclamation to me. I was so happy to learn of this news. At night, I made sure the door to the floor above the stairs was shut tight. I had purchased a lock and fastened it to the door to ensure the snake could not open it at any time while I was sleeping, and place his warm body in the bed next to mine. Did I say sleeping? I do not think I had a good night sleep for the first few nights after we moved in.

Every afternoon when the sun made it around our house, the snake would feel free to sun himself on a large stone slab outside the door leading into the kitchen. The snake did not bother us. He left us alone. But, I was bothered by the snake's presence.

There was a pitchfork leaning on the side of the barn door. Taking this in my hand, I bravely marched over to the snake. I wanted to remove the snake from the stone slab and keep him from getting back in the house. Right, like I was going to win?

Well, as I slowly moved closer to the snake, he started moving his way toward the foundation of the house and then he proceeded to slither his way up into and between the clapboards covering the house. What? Not happening!

After reassuring Emily Jane and Ryan that I was not going to kill the snake, they stood by and watched as I took the pitchfork and tried to wrap the tail end of the snake around the metal prongs. Once I had a grip on the snake, I twisted the bottom half of the body around the pitchfork and pulled with all my might. I could not believe how much strength was in the muscles on a snake's body. No matter how hard I tried, I could not stop him from continuing on his venture back into our basement. After this, I felt that he had just earned his right to the stone slab and I left him alone. From now on though, we were going to use the front door only!!

When the children napped in their beds upstairs, and as I looked out their bedroom window, I could see the snake taking his own rest on the stone slab. I was thankful for the door that became part of the flooring when placed over the top of the stairs. This gave me peace of mind at night as I knew the snake could not have a "sleepover" in our bedrooms anyway. He could have the whole basement!

I thought this "door over the stairs" was a very clever idea. I don't know who thought of this idea. But I liked it. My children were never going to break their necks at night because they had fallen down the stairs, because the snake couldn't get upstairs, and anyone who wanted to break into the house during the night couldn't get upstairs either. More importantly, this door gave us added security from any imaginary "Indians" that might have come around and wanted to attack us while we slept.

While living at this house, we were almost in total isolation from the rest of the world around us. I say "almost" because we did have daily visitors. We know about the snake, of course. Other common visitors were in the form of fisher cats, bears, deer, frogs, lots of grasshoppers and ANTS! The rural mail truck and our friends who lived up the street from us when we lived at the two brown houses were some of the human visitors that came our way.

Now, I could tolerate all the "National Geographical" finds around and about our house, but the visiting ants were NOT welcomed. They were the medium size black ants that made you want to scream a little if they crawled on you. In my case, I would have screamed a lot. But you already knew this. Here we go again. I sat at the kitchen table observing how they were able to enter the house and invade my kitchen. Of course, how did I not know they were "friends" of the snake who lived in the basement? When desiring to leave the snake's company, the ants decided to join Emily Jane, Ryan and I upstairs. They mainly kept to the borders of the kitchen. Still, their visits were not welcomed!

I was not in the mood to smack them as they appeared from under the tiniest little hole by the threshold of the door frame to the basement door. Instead, I decided to wrap this up quickly and with the aid of our Hoover vacuum I sucked them right up the nozzle of the hose and right into the removal, disposable bags. Afterwards, the children would take these bags (I did this ritual more than once) and sent them flying into the depths of the woods behind our house. The paper bags were biodegradable and the ant instead of having been whacked to death by a "crazy" screaming woman had another chance at life. I hope they liked camping! Did they need to borrow my tent?

Our house was situated on a very large parcel of land. There were miles of woodlands behind us. The children and I loved walking in the woods looking for tracks or to look for just about anything. As I write these words, I am thinking how I could be so afraid of the tiniest of God's creatures, yet I was not afraid to take a walk in the woods. One reason for this possibility was the fact that we took the dog with us. What dog did you say?

The DOG belonged to Charlie. The property owner of his residence did not allow dogs. He told Charlie this. The lease mentions "No Pets." Yet, Charlie still got himself a dog. After putting up with the dog barking for just so long, the owner made Charlie remove the dog from the property or he would have to move! Therefore, this white, tail wagging "horse" came to live with us. The children had pleaded with me to rescue their father's precious canine from the hands of the "evil" property owner. Hence, we now had a dog!

After a while, I did not mind having the dog around. He was a good dog. He stayed with the children and me when we were outside. During our walks into the woods, the dog kept his nose sniffing for any scents of something around us that might be of danger to us. He walked with his head high and tail straight up in the air, and did everything he could to make me want to like him.

Eventually, I did have great affection for the dog, and we became good friends. I even petted his head every now and then. This was genuine proof of my change of heart. The dog had already made friends with the children when they visited with their father. Ryan had tried to ride him as he would a horse many times. The dog did not seem to mind. Emily Jane continued to try to dress the dog like she used to dress her cat. The dog did not stay still long. Most of the time, she could not get him to sit still long enough for her to dress him in anything other than a hat. Still, this thoroughly purebred mutt became a welcomed member of our family.

We had a beautiful yard. On one side of the house is where the children played when they were outside. Under the enormous maple tree, I put their swing set. Behind the swing set, there was an old stone wall which I was glad was there. It gave the children an added boundary that protected them from accidentally, absent-mindedly having an urge to run in the road when chasing their balls or chasing after butterflies.

At the edge of the yard before it became a field area, there was a huge apple tree. When waking up early in the morning or right before we closed our eyes at bedtime, we would look out the bedroom window and wait for deer to pay a visit to the apple tree. Our viewing time was never wasted. Not long after we were on the lookout for deer, one or two would reward us with their presence.

There is something about nature that was helpful in reviving my tired soul. I didn't care what I may have experienced in my life, new blossoms on the flowers, a glimpse of an animal or their babies had a way of being able to soothe my troubles away. And, just like in the movies where there is musical accompaniment playing to support the picture's excitement, nature, too, has a music score of her own. The sounds of chirping birds, insects, the rustling of the leaves on a tree when the wind is blowing or the pitter patter of the tiny feet belonging to a mouse running around in the kitchen whet the appetite of what was coming our way for us to see or do. The oohs and amahs generated from my lips when I saw a deer or other animal seemed to erase anything stressful that was currently going on in my life.

Our front yard was not very big. Actually, there was just enough land to place our mailbox. When going out to get the mail one afternoon, I noticed a very large black "cat" crossing the road. His body was shinny and sleek, and his movements graceful. It was the first time I had ever seen a fisher cat. Although beautiful in many aspects, one look at his "ugly" face was all I needed to retreat back to the safety of our house. I prefer to view these natural beauties from behind the glass that covered the windows.

On the other side of the house, the darker side, is where the red and black raspberries grew. This area was loaded with raspberries. I could already taste the jam I had planned to make when the berries were nice and plump.

Beyond these was an overgrowth of the trees and mixed foliage, I declared this area would be off limits for us to explore. We did not venture out on this side because the mosquitoes, and at times the bears, favored this area and kind of claimed it as their own space! In the afternoon, the bears came often enjoyed their raspberry treats. I decided after seeing my first bear that the rasp-berries were all theirs! I made a mental note to buy the jam from the country store!

Further on past our home a little ways was a long dirt road. It was a primitive road. You took a risk when you traveled on this road. Having a spare tire in the car was a must. Eventually the road would lead you to a huge pond. The views around the pond were breathtaking. The wild life and vegetation added tremendously to this panoram-ic view. I did not care how many times we went to this pond, every visit opened our eyes to something new.

On hot days, the children donned their bathing suits and played in the shallow part of the pond while I sat on a chair by the edge of the water. The water was clear and the breeze brought relief from insects flying around me. If I sat in the sun, the bugs passing by did not seem to bother me as much. Either they preferred the shade over the sun or the sun was shining so brightly that it blinded my eyes from seeing the bugs. Either way, it was cool!

The pond was full of fish. If you looked down into the water, you could see little fish swimming around your feet and toes. Once in a while, a large fish could be seen and heard jumping out of the water to feast on a bug above them, and then it went splashing back into the water.

Ryan loved to bring a model boat that his father had put together. I attached a string to the boat, so Ryan could hold onto it as the small current bounced the boat all around him. All was quiet until Ryan lost his hold on the boat. Not good.

It did not take long for the current to pull the boat further and further out of our reach. It was too far out for Emily Jane to retrieve. I could not swim, and did not go in water above my knees. Trouble had found me again!

Ryan proceeded to scream. loudly. It did not matter how much or how long he was going to scream, I was not going in the water past me knees to get the boat. As Emily Jane and I sat on the beach trying to calm Ryan down, something miraculously happened right before our very eyes! The waves brought the boat back our way. After pulling the boat out of the water, I tied the boat to Ryan's wrist to prevent this drama from repeating itself. With the tears stopped and Ryan smiling again, the children headed back into the water to play.

When the screaming stopped, silence brought life back around to "normal." The butterflies, dragonflies and birds slowly returned to doing what they had been doing before all the drama started.

The children were thriving and loving their new place. I was working on my changes that I had set as goals to make. I also continued to study the Bible with the middle-aged couple who had come to visit me when we lived at the two brown houses. I was progressing and starting to see fruits for the changes I had been making. There were so many things I had to work on, and I was going to need the rest of my life to work out all my flaws and imperfections. But you knew that, right?

Other people who came around began noticing my changes, too. They could not believe I did not swear anymore, and that I went out of my way to be kind. Charlie also commented on my changes when he came for his visits with the children. He wanted to know "who" I was making these changes for. He was thinking that I was involved with another man. Was he kidding? He came around just to see if he could catch me hanging with another man. Eventually, he started coming around more often to spend time with Emily Jane and Ryan and, because I was being nice to him, he went out of his way to be kind to me, also. That was a "first" for him! See, people can change.

For once in my life, I could feel myself "regrouping" and taking control. Living did not seem to be all that bad despite my financial situation and the fact that we were pretty much void of other people in our lives. We did not have television reception or a telephone. Charlie had his own place, and I had not had any contact with any members of my family for some time. Life was peaceful. I loved it! Then, there came a knock at the front door!

The owners wanted their house back. Not quite thirty days after the children and I moved into the farm house, the property owner retired from his city employment in another state and imagine, "after all these years," twenty-five to be exact, "his wife finally agreed to relocate to their vacation home," the house we were renting, "to live permanently." This was a dream come true for him, but it would be a nightmare for me. He sheepishly asked me "did I mind giving up the farm house so he could live out his dream?" Would I mind finding another place to live?

However, I was fortunate again! When searching for a house to rent a couple of days later, I was able to locate a rental that was available in the same area that we were now living. We would be moving in two weeks. I was not in any hurry to pack again. Therefore, this time, I did not bother with all the cardboard boxes and tape routine. I just threw our belongings into the car and transferred them "as they were" to the new place. No unpacking was needed this way. Are we having fun yet? Let me guess!

# CHAPTER FOURTEEN
## The Big House

Welcome to the continuing saga of my life! We were in the sad process of moving our things from the farm house that had brought us so much comfort and into our new place, "The Big house." Another surprise would be waiting for us. You would not believe this, but the apartment complex that Charlie had been living in was destroyed by fire. All tenants needed to find alternative housing. The owner of the apartment building was not going to rebuild. Oh dear! Oh dear! Oh dear! Here we go again!

During the last several weeks and before the fire, Charlie had been hinting, without discretion, that he wanted to come back to live with us, you know, to be a family again. Normally, I would have had to give this lengthy consideration. I would have liked having had a little more time to meditate on his request before I gave Charlie my final decision. When considering his current situation, I felt pressured to give him an immediate answer. I offered to give Charlie one more chance. (I know what you are thinking, you don't have to say it. I already know. If this isn't evidence of strong code-pendency I don't know what else it can be, other than STUPID)!

So, almost a year to the date that Charlie and I had separated, he was now moving in with us again! Not so fast, mister! There was something he had to do first! He would have to find a new home for his dog, the one I had babysat for him while living at the farm house. The newest landlords did not want animals. He was very firm when he said, "NO," when I had asked him if he allowed pets. Since I was hoping to be able to stay living in this place for some time and wanted to start off on the right foot with our new landlords, the dog was sent packing. Three pairs of eyes and their stares were planting "land minds" in my brain, and they were ready to set them off if I did not allow the dog to stay. Unfortunately, there were not a lot of rental options in our area. I chose to put my foot down and appease our new landlord. I felt it was more important that we have a place to live. I was beginning to find my back bone.

Two days after we moved into the big house, the honeymoon period was over and, of course, Charlie was back to doing his old things. Music was still his primary focus in life (Did Charlie ever focus on anything else)? He was also lazy and still irresponsible. Then, wouldn't you know it. He quit his job at the group home. He claimed he was "burnt out" and needed time to get himself "together." He needed to "regroup" after the fire and after having lost most of his belongings. You can imagine how he was beside himself with joy after sifting through items that remained usable after the fire, and found that all his music equipment escaped damage. Wonderful! After all, we couldn't be without thousands of guitar straps and microphone stands, now could we?

This was not going to work for me. The agreement we had before he moved back in with us was that he was going to pay the rent and provide for our daily needs. Counterproductively, since he quit his job, I knew that this was not going to help him keep his end of our bargain! I began to have major flashbacks around my life with Charlie before we had separated and I wanted to torture (in a long and slow fashion) myself for allowing Charlie back in my life. I became severely depressed when I realized that I had made another huge mistake. I had to stop being weak. I also had to stop this cycle of abuse and the dysfunction from continuing into my children's generation. I did not want them to suffer because I was not emotionally strong as a result of the scars of my childhood and now because of my relationship with Charlie. I knew things were going to have to change, but how these changes would come about I did not know. I was clueless. All the while, our home life was becoming more and more toxic. I began looking harder to find solutions. I began to reach out in prayer, and I just knew this would be a step in the right direction.

Constant contradictions and discord developed between Charlie and I. We still had the same problems we had before he left. All of these problems stemmed around money, music, his needs, and his wants. I, on the other hand, still had my own list of priorities such as needing to put the children first and making sure they had their needs, keeping them safe and fed, and needing to pay our bills, mainly the rent! Our daily battles continued. Yet, I was finding refuge in prayer and reaching out more for God's direction and guidance. I will admit I needed His help.

Still living in isolation with employment options in the area still at "zero to none," there was not a whole lot I could do as I sat back to see what Charlie was going to do about fulfilling his end of the bargain. I decided to put the ball in his court and see if he could make something happen. I already knew that this situation like all the other ones I had to face in my life was going to mean disappointment for me in the end. I wasn't letting Charlie off the hook this time. For the last several years, he consistently blamed me for all our problems and he seemed to have this need to remind me that I was not a good person, mother or wife. So, I sat back this time to see what the big talking, loud mouth and all-of-a-sudden "family man" was going to do. I wanted to see if he had any better ideas than I had come up with over the years. I wanted to see if he could do better at stretching the money we had coming into the house to cover all our necessities. I knew there was much more I could learn! I say, "okay big fella, put your money where your mouth is!"

We were not off to a good start. The big house was not in the greatest condition. It had been empty for quite some time before I came around to see about renting it. The house was old, the rooms were dark and dull, and major work needed to be done on it to make it acceptable and before we made it our new living quarters. This house was a major setback after having come from the bright and clean, peaceful rooms we had enjoyed at the farmhouse. I knew I was going to be extremely unhappy living here.

The outside of the house was not very pretty. Previous renters had left trash all over the backyard and the grass had turned to "seeds" which meant it had grown very tall. Before the children could play safely in this area, I needed to clean it up and make sure there wasn't anything hiding in the "jungle" that could hurt the children. I needed to clear out any broken bottles, rusting tin cans, or you know, snakes or other crawling critters! The children and I raked and tidied the yard as best as we could. In time the backyard was up to my standards and I allowed Emily Jane and Ryan to once again to play outside.

We now had a clean house and a clean yard but it still wasn't looking good for any of us with Charlie back in our lives. Yet, like all the other times in my life, I would continue to make the best of it and put my best foot forward. Emily Jane and little Ryan still needed to feel secure and needed help adjusting to their new home. I had to help them accept our situation and make it appear "normal" for them.

After we had our place set up, it did not take much effort on my part to get us back on track and falling back into our regular routine we started while living at the farm house. Things we had been doing before Charlie had come back. I wanted the children to know—and feel—that the only thing that had changed when we moved, was the location. I wanted everything else to stay the same.

Reading was one of our favorite ways to pass time. We were still attending the daycare center. I volunteered a couple of days a week so that Emily Jane and her brother Ryan could have opportunities to be with other children. I was hoping it would help them with any bad thoughts they might have had around our moving again or just in general.

Having our baths, getting ready for bed, and sleeping were also other activities in our routine that I enjoyed. After putting the children to bed and placing the blanket over my shoulders in my own bed, it always left me with a wonderful feeling. It would mean I had survived another day and my children were still enduring with me.

Charlie set up his "music" room downstairs and, most of the time, it was off limits to everyone but him. This was his sanctuary, his man cave. He set up his speakers, put his stereo on a bookshelf and surrounded this with demo tapes and other stuff. He also had to have silence in the house so he could concentrate on the songs he was writing. With two young children, he wasn't asking too much was he? Please, give me a break!

Don't get me wrong, Charlie did have some music talent. He had a nice singing voice and could play guitar. However, there comes a time in life where you have to grow up. After twenty-something years of trying one thing and it is still not working for you or it is not generating money to support yourself and your family (or the family he had created before us, another story, another book), you really should try your hand at something else. Don't you think? Charlie could not be content in life unless he was playing his guitar. I understood his feelings to some degree, as at one time when living in the green house, my guitar had been my best friend. Charlie's life was all about music and anything else that he allowed to filter in now and then where fringe benefits he received from being part of our family. Ladies, be careful when dating a musician. Their poetry is delightful and rock n' roll dreams sound super exciting, but their "follow through" does not have good odds. Take it from me.

I, on the other hand, was not very hard to please. I was content with having sustenance and covering. I was happy to endure each day despite the hole I had dug for myself. I worked hard to make daily life pleasant for the children. I kept the depression hidden within myself and directed my fears and aspirations to God. I gave up trying to make Charlie happy. Nothing made Charlie happy other than music, of course. Charlie was just not happy with himself. I did not have the ability to make Charlie happy no matter how hard I tried. It was not going to happen. Questions were invading my mind again around the life I was currently living. Would Charlie just keep fathering children and never feel the need to support them or have a part in raising them? What kind of person was he inside that he felt it was okay to keep creating babies and then not provide for them? Would I ever have the answers to these questions? Would I be able to accept the reality of who he was and move on if necessary?

Lo and behold, Charlie interjected a great surprise and got himself a job. This was stunning, a real curve ball. Could it be true? During the long days he was gone, the children and I kept busy around our house. We played memory games and spent time doing things with our hands like making cookies or special treats. When we went for our daily walks, we studied our surroundings and looked for anything we saw that was interesting to our eyes. Entertainment was in the form of a pretty flower, an interesting bug, or just admiring the colors on whatever grew around us. We did not need video games or the internet. This was good as we still did not have cable in our area yet. The children and I were easy to please and what we did was cost efficient!

Emily Jane and her brother Ryan were good children. Both were smart, too. Emily Jane was reading before she started school. She used her playtime to teach her brother how to read and helped him to learn his numbers. They played well together most of the time. They had their moments as all children do.

When Charlie had the day off from work, we broke up our daily routine by going to the pond. Charlie would fish and Emily Jane and Ryan would play in the water. Occasionally, I did some fishing, too. Or, I should say, I tried to fish. I spent a great deal of my time trying to get the fishing line and hook unstuck from the undergrowth in the water or out of the tree behind me. I could not get the hang of casting my line into the water. To be truthful, mostly, I spent my time swatting at things that flew around me. Not much had changed in my being able to tolerate bugs. Actually nothing had! I can proudly say I had not lost my ability to scream loudly either. I still had it even after all the screaming I had done over the last few years! GIVE ME FIVE!

I was not your "eagle scout" kind of person. The only time I enjoyed being outdoors is when I was walking from the front door of the house to the car door. I considered it very admirable of me to spend time outside for my children's sake. I did my best not to let my phobias rub off on them. Just because I was afraid of the water or bugs or did not like something, it did not mean Emily Jane or Ryan had to be afraid of these things or dislike them too. In fact, I encouraged them to do anything they wanted to do. I wanted them to reach for the sky, and not have to keep their feet on the ground because of my fears.

The winter months were passing by very quickly. Having to purchase fuel to heat this big house was eating any money I set aside for rent. Charlie's paycheck could be stretched in just so many different ways. A greater portion of the money went toward gasoline for the car. His job was forty miles away from home. Any remaining funds were set aside for the children's needs: food, clothing and heat. The rent always took a backseat to our current needs.

Heating the big house reminded me of the time I was living at the white house on top of the hill. It did not matter how high the temperature was set on the thermostat, I could never seem to get the house to stay warm. I was constantly trying to adjust the thermostat to generate more heat. It always felt like there was a slight chill still in the air once the furnace stopped. Many times, we had to make a decision to purchase fuel or pay our rent. Purchasing fuel always won out. It was one of the coldest winters I had lived through in my lifetime. Sadly, we started falling behind in our rent.

Consequently, in the spring, the owners of the big house demanded the back rent, which we did not have, of course. It felt as if I was reliving the situation we had at the three-bedroom trailer. Same tune just a different "time" or is it rhythm?

The owners were fair and allotted us a couple of weeks to clear our belongings off of their property. We packed most items into boxes, keeping out only the necessary items we would need when moving to our next place. The rest of the items were going to be stored. We were downsizing as we were moving to a campground. This time, we would have to make do without a camp trailer. And this time, along with my dear husband, I now had

TWO children. I started to prepare my heart and soul to help me face the continuing challenges that kept coming my way. I figured if I accepted these ongoing challenges as a permanent part of my life, it would make enduring them a little easier.

# CHAPTER FIFTEEN
## The Custom Deluxe Van

This time, moving to the campground was not as bad as I had anticipated it was going to be. In fact, instead of a micro-sized tent or camper, we had upgraded to a big, spacious, custom deluxe, Ford economy van. I organized our "home on wheels" in a way that would allow our "things" (such as the First Aid Kit, pots and pans, snacks, cooler, clothing, bedding, Ryan's immense collection of matchbox cars and Tonka toys and of course, all of Emily Jane's thousands of books) to be easily accessible when we needed these items. The van was also organized in a way I would "remember" where I had put each item! Everything had its own purpose and place. I did not need to give myself a ranting pep rally size cheer this time either. Enduring was all in the attitude. This was my new motto! It helped that I was a lifelong pro at surviving difficult situations. I had experience in this department!

I learned many favorable shortcuts that helped to make camp life doable from having previously camped for the summer after leaving the A-Frame chalet. This time, I insisted that we set up our campsite next to the washrooms. This was a stellar idea as you can imagine the added convenience. Surprisingly, the washrooms were clean and they offered splendid showers. Several times during the day, I let the children take a shower just for the fun of it. It kept them clean, cool and washed off anything that did not belong on them! Just outside the washroom doors was another added bonus that helped make camp life a little bit more tolerable. There was an area set aside for washing dishes with HOT WATER! Did you hear me right? HOT WATER! I'm in, sign me up!

The ground area around of the washroom was paved. A roof overhead covered and shaded this spot. It became a "play" area for the children in the park when it rained. On rainy days, Emily Jane and Ryan rode their hot wheels here and all the while keeping dry. This was a nice, complementary fringe benefit, which was a contributing factor when we were choosing a campground. We used this covered area to the max as it rained for TWENTY NINE days out of the first thirty-one days we were there. I am serious! Despite all the rain, I still had all my hair, and my children and I were somehow having the time of our lives. It felt as if we had actually gone on a family vacation. We were having fun! I mean, what was there not to enjoy, right?

Another amenity offered at this campground was the many open fields in which to choose a campsite and plenty of room in between each site allowing us a bit of privacy while we were there. This offered a varied view and kept us enjoying the change of pace. It was almost like camping on the Creator's front lawn with the trees behind us and rolling fields at our disposal. The bonus of fewer trees, I soon learned, was that it meant there were fewer bugs. Fewer, is good! Fewer, is VERY good! Fewer, meant that there would be a whole lot less shrieking on my part, and fewer potential heart attacks for Charlie! Charlie never did know when or what would cause me to scream and often would be totally unprepared and very surprised when the screaming started! After coming downing for a landing, his eyes would glance over to where I was to make sure I was okay and then he would go back to reading his newspaper, strumming his guitar or whatever he had been doing. It also meant that the children did not have to come running to check on their "Momma" to make sure she was okay a million times a day. After learning it was "just a bug" that sent me into a screaming rage, the children went right back to what they had been doing. Everyone was getting used to the routine. Yes, fewer bugs would be good for serenity!

Since it was still early in the season when we first set up our campsite, we had most of the park to ourselves during the week. The children ran around like wild animals and played endlessly. Emily Jane was beyond clever and imaginative and could occupy her little brother for hours in her treasured land of "make believe." (Possibly an inherited trait she got from her grandmother)! This was a great source of joy for me to observe seeing them get along and having a relationship with one another. I marveled at how unique Emily Jane was and her little brother, too, as he copied everything his sister did. Ryan just wanted to be her cookie cutter, spitting image.

The park's maintenance crew kept the grounds manicured and clean. It really was a nice place to camp. I would recommend it to anyone wanting to find a nice family "get-a-way" for a weekend! Also worthy of noting, today as adults, Emily Jane and her brother Ryan still prefer living outdoors and can't wait for any opportunity to camp out. Emily Jane, unlike her mother, does not scream when a bug approaches. More often than not, she will pick the bug up and calmly place it out of harm's way. Ryan doesn't seem to mind bugs either way but enjoys camping out without "Momma" as it is much quieter this way.

While Emily Jane and Ryan played games or rode their hot wheels, I was learning to master the art of cooking on an outside grill. Our meals ventured beyond hamburgers and hotdogs. I was even successful in learning how to use a camp oven which was placed on the wire grate on the grill. I could now make meatloaf, cookies, cakes and casseroles. I could make just about anything now, just like I could have had I been cooking in a real kitchen. Bobby Flay would have been truly impressed. Yes, indeed, things were beginning to look up.

Charlie, on the other hand, was feeling the pinch as he was trying to master the new roles he had taken on. He was daringly trying his hands at being the husband, father and employee all at one time. He was now traveling over sixty-five miles, one way, to work. This had to have been a major shock to his system. I'm sure of it. He was up bright and early in the morning and did not get back to the campground until late afternoon or early evening. These were long days for him and he was getting tired. Other than for a few beers here and there, he did not have much of an emotional outlet and he was like an animal caught in a trap. In other words, there wasn't an electric outlet for him to plug in his electric guitars! There was no music room; there was no television set or telephone for that matter. There was not much in the way of words anyone could say to make Charlie feel better about his situation. It was going to be a very long and depressing summer for him.

I am sure Charlie had a lot to think about on his long drives to and from work each day. Before we moved to the campground, I informed Charlie that he had until the last month of summer to find us an appropriate place to live. I wanted the family in a home with walls before the start of the next school session. I also wanted to have the full benefits of indoor living when winter made her appearance! I thought this was a fair request. As we were living in such a severely remote area with only one car, one of us had to work while the other stayed home and watched the children. Charlie chose working over the latter option. I was feeling trapped in this situation. I wanted to work to help out financially as I knew it would help make our life a little bit easier. I wanted to alleviate some of the stresses Charlie now had piled up on his back. Now, I was the one feeling like a hungry bear in a cage! Wait a minute. I wonder how much Mrs. Bear around the corner from us would have charged to babysit a couple hours a day? Now, there is a possibility. Why had I not thought of this before?

I feel the need to remark at this point on how little or no contact Charlie had with his own family. He had several older brothers and a sister who had done well for themselves. His brothers and his sister did not approve of the way Charlie led his "imaginary" rock star life. I say "imaginary" because they way Charlie talked about music to others and his part he had in it you might have thought he went on "tour" every six weeks and was raking in the money! In reality, he played a gig a couple of times a year and spent the rest of the year PRACTICING! Charlie's family also did not approve of the way he managed his finances, his life style, etc. In other words, they did not agree with the way he handled anything in his life. At points in his life when he hit rock bottom (like right now for instance) or when he was struggling to some degree because of some other reason, they did not offer any assistance or seem to have any interest in helping Charlie in any way shape or form. So despite the fact that we had all their names, addresses and phone numbers in our "Address Book," nobody called so this appeared to be a waste of ink on paper. They never even attempted to step in and try to help us "role play" solutions to our problems. The fact that Charlie was presently living in a campground with his wife and two children didn't seem to alarm Charlie's family members in any way. They kind of went on with their own lives as Charlie was seemingly always in some sort of trouble and always seemed to manage to keep himself from drowning.

Charlie's parents had passed away a long time ago and, when they had been alive, they had definitely considered Charlie the "black sheep" of their Irish, conventional, blue collar family. The move to the A-Frame chalet after leaving the house at the bottom of the school hill caused him to drift from the cousins and nephews he had been close with when he and I had met. They had all left their young ways and started families and businesses of their own. In other words, they had settled into a life applicable to their aging. They were now living "grown up" lives. Charlie still wanted to party. This was no longer amusing for his family as he was now well into his 30's and had fathered four children in total that needed to be clothed and fed and, oh yes, loved! These thoughts must have made for some long, intense, lonely drives for Charlie as he daily traveled to and from work.

Charlie also needed to plan ahead as to how he was going to provide for us as he would be responsible for paying all our household needs this time until we were able to settle into an area closer to town where I could again find work while Emily Jane was in school and Ryan was in daycare in the fall. There were no more free rides for him. His tokens were all used up. I had told him that I would find ways to keep expenses down and would be content with just having our very basic needs. I did not need jewelry or fancy cars. I didn't need to go on vacations. I felt that after living at TWO campgrounds, I had all the vacations I needed to last a lifetime. He just had to hold a steady job and get us into a home with four walls and close enough to civilization so that I could walk to get our supplies when he had the car. Oh, and NO more dogs that we were not supposed to have in our homes as outlined in our lease! Emily Jane and Ryan took it too hard when they had to say good-bye to their pets. Their little animal-loving hearts didn't need to say any more good-byes to their furry, four-legged friends. Daily living was emotional enough!

I was not trying to be mean to Charlie and I was not angry with him or trying to get even with him when I confronted him with my list of ultimatums before we moved to the campground, but I needed him to prove to me that he wanted to be with us and that he would do his part to keep us together as a family. Music was nice, but family was higher on my list of importance. I needed him to prove it was on the top of his list, too.

Unfortunately, as summer was winding down, so was the reality of any proof that Charlie had a plan to rectify our living situation. He was feeling even more trapped then I was as a hungry bear in a cage and he was simply miserable. It was not the life he wanted to live. He could have fooled me? He had made so many empty promises to me over the years. (And I quote: "I have changed," or "I will make more changes." The promise I liked hearing the best, "I will provide." Then came the "Emily Jane needs a brother or sister; I don't want her to grow up an only child, blah, blah, blah…" I fell for his promises each time, hook, line and sinker). He wanted to have the world given to him on a "silver" platter. Charlie had a different outlook now that he had to pay his way. This did not help our relationship. He became more caustic. He grew more insufferable every day.

He was not physically abusive but his words may just as well been soul-shattering bombs. His words destroyed any leftovers of my self-esteem and zapped me of the energy I needed to keep enduring. The mental anguish lingered longer than some of the trials I experienced in my yesteryears. In those days, at least Irene, David and their children went home after the weekends and I had the week to regroup. Now, it did not seem like I had time to recuperate from the pains I felt from his harsh words before I would be subjected to his demeaning criticism and put downs over and over again. I was depressed.

August was fast approaching and the weather was already turning frigid. I began to notice some unacceptable inconsistencies in Charlie's routine. I thought that perhaps he might have been looking around after work for our next home. He had not been. This was not the reason for his coming home late. The real reason was that he had instead been going out with the "boys" for drinks after work. Liking his new outlet, he began coming home later and later each evening. Drinks weren't free, so he was also coming home with fewer resources in his pockets. Oh dear! We were going to end up having to build an igloo if something didn't happen soon!

As we only had the one car at this time, I would wait all day for Charlie to return from work, so that I could go into town to do our laundry and get the supplies we needed for the following day when he would be gone with the car again. His not coming home in a timely fashion was evidence that he was not thinking about his family or their needs. He was thinking only about Charlie and his needing to "escape" reality. Not Good!

Since he was not proving to me that he was out looking for a place, and his time was running out, I started seeking out my own outlets for my children and me as to where we would move when the summer ended. I was done playing games. I had to take the deck of cards into my hands now. I was shuffling the deck and I would determine the next card I would play. After playing my final "card" in this game though, I was going to BURN THE DECK!

I had been praying for direction and finally felt sure I was receiving some answers. Mercy had shone itself in the form of an acquaintance and her husband noticing our situation and seeing me with two children still living at the campground. Evidence around us made it clear that an early winter was fast approaching. This couple made me the kindest offer. I accepted their offer. Thank God. Tearfully as I had planned, after Charlie left for work on the last day of the month of August, I packed up a few of our things and this lovely woman came to the campground to take the children and me to our new place. When Charlie came back to the campground that night, he was shocked to find that we had flown the coop. He was enraged when he saw that we had left and, when he was able to locate where we had gone, he actually came to our new place and demanded that I, we, come back. NOW! He was furious, threatening and hateful, but I stood my ground. It was not going to happen this time. He was never going to put our needs over his wants. In my heart, I wanted to give in to him, I wanted him to be a changed person, but he wasn't. At this point I was beyond convinced that he would never change and do his part so we could stay together as a family. With God's help, I closed our new front door. The children and I would be staying at our new place without him!

At this time, I knew that in all my years with Charlie (almost seven) I had done just about everything I could think of to keep a relationship with him. Because we had Emily Jane and Ryan, I tried even harder to keep us together as a family. I can look back now and know that I did not fail in my efforts.

Charlie could never look back on my time with him and not be able to truly admit that I had gone beyond the call of duty with him, as his girlfriend, his wife and as the mother of his children. He would never be able to say I left him because things had gotten bad. My whole relationship with him had been bad from the start. I went down with him in every hole we had dug for ourselves. However, his continued refusal to accept his responsibility and put his family first in his life finally sunk the ship. I had left Charlie. This time leaving Charlie would be for good. I inhaled a big breath, and then I let out the longest ever sigh of relief. I had come to grips and accepted the fact that I had not made many good choices concerning my relationship with Charlie. But, I also knew that I could walk away this time and not have any regrets. I needed to move forward for my sake and for the sake of my children.

My children, Emily Jane and Ryan, were the glue that kept me together and the cement that kept me trying to be better and do better. I was determined to allow our future to soften the negative situations that we had already faced and to work on building happier memories for us. In all that I had been through since leaving the house at the bottom of the school hill, I can truly say, I had never, ever, ever stopped being a mother. I had always been there for my children. I truly loved them with all my heart. So despite all the downsides of my relationship with Charlie, I saw my children as a gift. They were precious to me. My children were my life. They kept me on the winning end and kept me determined to survive whatever would come our way.

# CHAPTER SIXTEEN

## *The House*
## *At the Edge of Paradise*

*T*he lovely married couple had offered me the use of their fabulous house situated in a more civilized area. In other words, a place that was not so isolated from the real world and having real world conveniences around us. This couple would be leaving soon to travel to one of their other homes out of state. They asked me if I would housesit for them and take care of their birds and plants, and watch over their large estate. It felt like the Red Sea had just been parted before my very eyes! The children were overcome with excitement, and their eyes came alive as they anticipated the adventures that awaited them. I welcomed this unexpected opportunity and accepted their gracious offer. As planned as I already noted, at the end of August, all of our meager, earthly possessions were picked up at the campground and brought to our new home.

Emily Jane was almost six and a half years old and her brother Ryan had just turned four a few weeks before our move. The children loved the fact that we were going to be babysitting for the birds (ducks, geese, and peacocks) and were eager to help me care for them. There were several good things to note about our babysitting these birds. First, the children and I loved the birds and they knew us. Secondly, these birds, or rather soon to be "pets" had permission from the owners to live on the property.

It would not be so sweet for Charlie though. He could not get over the fact that I left him. He came to our new residence several times in the next couple of days and he was not happy. In his fury, he demanded over and over again that the children and I go back with him to the campground. I tried to reason with him and reminded him about our talk before we went to the campground from the big house. Still, the more I tried to reason with him the angrier he got with me. Having this wakeup call did not sit well with him. I stood firm with my choice but my heart did weaken. It was hard on me beyond words to see Charlie so depressed. I could see the tears welling up around the whites of his eyes. The dams were holding back his "hidden" tears, tears that were not meant for anyone else to see. I knew these tears all too well. Looking back on my own experiences in life, I knew that these tears held pains and sorrows. Secret tears, the tears of true feelings held within. Only the person shedding them knew the reasons why and how much they had been hurting. Seeing these "hidden" tears in Charlie's eyes made me somewhat confused. What was he really feeling? What did he really want? I had to stop my thoughts and shake off any emotions I had around his feelings. It would not be good for me to dwell on them. It would just extend the rollercoaster ride I had been on and I was feeling the need to stop the ride now and I was eager and ready to move on.

Still though, when the couple recognized that it was difficult for me to see Charlie in such an unfortunate situation, they, too, had a change of heart and offered to allow Charlie the opportunity to come stay with us while we were house sitting. They had strong rules and regulations behind his being able to come and reconcile with us at the house. They said I would be the one to make the final decision. Feeling sorry for Charlie, I have to admit, I did weaken and I told Charlie about the couple's offer and the rules behind their offer. I wanted to know how he was feeling about joining us. There would be no room in their exquisite home for excess music garb and they didn't want his whole band using their home as a rehearsal studio. Instead of appreciating their kind offer, he was enraged. NO ONE #@#! #!!@, was going to tell him what he could and could not do! It was plain and simple. His negative and abusive response ended our conversation after which I walked away from him and came into the house shutting the door behind me! Well, so much for my "hidden" tears theory. I took another long, deep breath.

Charlie spent the next couple of months traveling to work from his place at the campground and soon was able to find an alternate place where he could live. Eventually, he moved in with one of the "guys" he had been going out for drinks with nightly while we waited for him to come home from work. "He" turned out to be a "she!" When he told me about his new "friend, he grinned and exclaimed saucily that "she" had **money!** He was all set for now. He had a new place to live, a woman to care for his needs and a woman who had money to pay his way. He hit the jackpot for sure! Unbelievable! How does he do it?

Now that Charlie and I did not live together anymore, I took control of my own life. Because of the emotional impact that the separation had on the children, I set ground rules about his visitations with the Emily Jane and Ryan. I also set rules for when he could call them on the telephone. Charlie never did like to play by someone else's rules. He certainly was not going to let a "woman" tell him what to do at this time either! Clearly, Charlie did what he wanted to do. It did not matter to him what the results would be or how his actions affected others. He was going to do things his way and his way only!

It did not take Charlie long though to "adjust" his way of thinking and conform to my way of thinking when deciding whether or not to comply with my ground rules concerning the children! Having missed a few opportunities to visit with his children because he did not listen when I spoke to him, he did come around after a while and see the need to do things my way. If he wanted to speak with the children during the week or visit them on the weekends, he was going to have to toe the line. This was my house now. He lost his ability to "govern" the household or have any "input" on what went on inside my house when I left him.

The house at the edge of paradise was on a beautiful piece of property. The house was built in the middle 1800's and had all the charm belonging to this time period. The slanting walls on the second floor, a claw foot tub, milk houses, barn and chicken coop were all adorned in the décor of this era. It reminded me of the white house at the top of the hill, only a little newer. If only the walls could spit out the history that went on in and around the home. I would have listened with interest.

To the left side of the house was a garage. The next building after the garage was an old milk house which was still wearing the original red paint. All the birds lived in the milk house during the winter months. A light hanging from the ceiling would warm the chickens, peacocks, ducks and geese during the colder days and nights. The housing protected them from the snow, wind and rain. The children and I would lay fresh hay down every day for their feet. This helped to keep them dry from any moisture forming around them and guaranteed that they would not be "frozen statues" when we came to feed them in the morning. Thinking back on the dead fish hanging from the fishing pole thing, I did everything in my power to keep these new "pets" alive and happy!

Behind the milk house was the long driveway that took you to the back of the home. This is where the couple had their amazing garden. They grew many different vegetables and flowers. Their garden could have been highlighted in a magazine; in fact I think it had been. It was so perfectly planted and arranged. They had built a fence around the garden to keep the deer from eating their produce.

The chicken coop to the left of the garden is where the chickens spent the nights and rainy days before the snow began to fall. After feeding the chickens, we would check for any eggs they may have left in their nest or around the property. Thanks to special chicken feed and "Cheerios" we did not have a short supply of eggs at this house. The hens and the geese did their job well. We were grateful to have these eggs. We had eggs in our potato salad, egg salad, eggs in our chef salads, scrambled eggs, fried eggs, occasional omelets and we used these eggs in our cookies, cakes and muffins. It would not be hard to guess that we had eggs coming out of our ears! But, we loved eggs! Yes we did!

To the left of the chicken coop was a pond. This pond was really just a large hole in the ground that would catch any rain water that ran down from the hill above it. We kept it mowed around the edges of the water so we could see anything that moved when we took our daily walks. Yes, we still had sticks in our hands and yes, we still hit the ground before we took each step. And, just like at the two brown houses, all kinds of creepy things jumped into the water and out of our way as we took our walks around the pond. There were many frogs and snakes for sure. I did not take the time to examine everything that moved around us. I had lost the "wanting to discover" enthusiasm when we left the campground! I just kept hitting the ground with my stick as I moved forward. Fast! I did not scream as much anymore as my vocal chords were kind of worn out from my life's experiences over the past seven years. I needed to keep any ounce of sanity I still had left which meant keeping my voice so I could be sure people and things around me could hear me if I had anything to say or if I wanted to SCREAM! Did I ever really have any sense of normalcy in my life? There was no doubt in my mind. I knew the answer to this question. By now, I am sure you knew the answer, too.

To the right side of the chicken coop, just past the vegetable and flower garden, was another pond. The spring waters that flowed into this pond kept its water fresh. The owners kept it stocked with rainbow trout which could and did swim here. It was at this pond where the geese and the few mallard ducks we had in our care spent most of their time during the day. The children and I spent hours watching them swim around as we took our walks around this pond. And yes, with our sticks. There was no deviating in our routine when it came to sticks. Sticks were a must have! We hit the ground with our sticks, took a step or two and watched for anything that moved. Then, we proceeded to repeat the cycle. Nature tested me out a few times with her surprises. But it was okay. I shook off any fear or bugs that landed on me, and I was able to quickly regroup. It never ceased to amaze me even after all these years!

A stone wall bordered the property edges in the back

and in part of the property in the front of the house. This is where the strawberries had been planted and grew. The ducks made their daily walks to this wall and had their sweet berry treats after which they waddled back to the pond. Occasionally a chipmunk or two darted in and out between the spaces in the stone wall. Fencing bordered the rest of the front edging of the property. Flowers bordered these fences. Orange and yellow tiger lilies, red tulips, white and purple violets and some kind of blue flower. Anyway, they made the landscaping all so very pretty!

On the other side of the fence had to be the oldest butternut tree still standing in the area. It was huge. When walking on this side of the yard during the fall, you had to watch where you planted your feet. Stepping on one of these fuzzy coated nuts might cause you to lose your footing when they rolled under your feet as you walked. This could mean that you might find yourself flat on your back and on the ground. I wonder how I knew that. Yes, yes, yes, you are right if you guessed that I had fallen a time or two!

Life at this house was going to be peaceful. It had all that was necessary to make us want to be part of the scenery. At night, we would go down to the pond just before the sun set and we fed the fish their special food. A few seconds after throwing the food towards the water, the trout would literally jump out and "catch" the food in their mouths before it landed in the water. Even though, we never caught the fish, the couple who owned the house enjoyed eating one of their fish cooked on the grill every now and then. After the fishing derby problem with Emily Jane, we opted to just look at them swim in the pond. Our taste buds never went beyond desiring fish other than what came out of a tin can!

During the sunny part of the day, the geese, ducks and the peacocks sunned themselves and looked around the yard for any "natural" treats they could find to eat. They would pick at their feathers, shake their bodies and fluff themselves up. Nature had her own way of keeping them looking like they should without all the hustle and bustle of a beauty salon or spa! Watching these birds go about their daily lives was the best affordable entertainment around! And, it was free!

We often sat outside on the back deck during the course of the day and watched for any animals that might come to visit us. We also watched for any other geese or ducks that flew over the area and checked into the "inn" for the night at our pond. We watched to see if any deer would venture out of the woods behind the ponds to have a refreshing sip of cool pond water.

When we started eating our meals at the lawn table on the back deck, the "birds" would come around and would not go away until we gave them a "treat." Just like dogs! The geese usually came first. We kept a large box of "Cheerios" by the back door. A few handfuls of these tasty oats were all they needed. After eating their treats, they would waddle back down the hill to the pond. The chickens took over where the geese left off. They did not go away until they received their daily dosage of the toasty treats. The peacocks were not as trusting as these other birds, but eventually these, too, came for their mid-afternoon snack. All the while, they would look at us as if to say "thank you!" If you are interested, peacocks also enjoy eating pieces of hot dogs and rice! Make sure it's cooked wild rice or brown rice. I don't suggest feeding them any white rice as it tends to be too starchy.

I learned a lot about the birds as I watched them while living at this house. When the male peacock screeched, his mate would come running from wherever she was to be with him. The children and I became good at imitating this screech and when we "called" the male would screech back at us. In the fall, we followed the male around the yard and picked up his feathers as they fell off his body. Soon we had peacock feathers displayed all over our house.

The male goose took the lead in his realm. When he honked or when he started running and took to the air, the others followed him. They did not think about why he honked or why he wanted them to run? They just followed what he was doing. It simply meant either he wanted to have a meeting while they swam in the water or there was an enemy lurking somewhere nearby. Few dogs dared to come into the yard every now and then, but if they did, the air rifle was nearby for me to use. A few shots to the ground around them sent these occasional enemies out of our yard and back to where they came from.

There was so much for us to do at this new home. We visited the beaver pond, which was located in the middle of the woods behind our house. In the spring when the ice on the beaver pond melted, the couple brought their mallard ducks to their summer "home." Every day, we walked down to the beaver pond to make sure the mallards were still around and we would bring them a bowl of feed for them to eat.

There was a special kind of peace that came over me when I sat there on a bed of needles that had fallen between the rows of pine trees. This bed of needles was so thick and so soft, it dared you to want to lay your head down and rest. (However so tempting, I was not quite ready to test this theory out yet)! It looked as if these pine needles had never felt the prongs of a metal rake. Their piles left on the ground provided a soft chair for anyone who wanted to sit for a while. The area was almost untouched by human hands or their trash. It was almost—almost pure.

Occasionally, we were able to watch the beavers as they built their homes that would dam up areas around the pond to assure water would always be there for them. There was so much life around them and for us to see as we sat there taking it all in. Quiet times like these made me wonder where man had gone wrong. I knew from the things I saw with my own eyes at this pond that this was how God wanted us to live. Not the life I was presently experiencing or what I saw on television or in the newspapers. This was the "real" life. I was certain of it. It was all so calming, refreshing and beautiful. We had to force ourselves to go back to our own home after each visit.

In the latter part of the fall, I received word that my father had passed away. At first, I was not able to respond. As I repeated the words, "your father has passed away" in my mind, the tears began to pour out from my heart. The reality that I wouldn't see my father again (at least at the present time) struck me hard. I had never told him I loved him. I didn't know if I did love him. My parent's drama had robbed me of this opportunity. Still though, I did not have the time or the emotional stamina to focus on what I could have had or should have had. Not right now anyway. I had two growing children to walk through the changes they were facing at this time in their life. I pulled myself together, took a very deep breath and I buried any thoughts of my father back into the reservoir of my soul. This is how it had to be at least for now.

We were living at the top of the mountain now. This tended to make the winter's air feel ten degrees colder. Something was different though. It was the fact that we had all of the heat we could dream of! Even though we had plenty of heat, thanks to the overhaul the house had just gotten from the owners, I had to think ahead and prepare for our needs especially if we should be snowed in for a few days. I always had the mind set to make sure we had food in the house and treats to get us through any hard times we might face. These winter months were rough on us, but they were not too tough for us to handle. We did get a lot of snow. One month, we were "blessed" with fifty-six inches. When I shoveled the snow in front of the house, I had to stack the shoveled snow "above" my head! It was piled about 8 feet or so high. Three feet over my head, whoa!

When we shoveled the snow, we had to shovel a path from the main road to our fuel tank and from the front of the house to the back of the house. Of course, we had to excavate a long path to where the "birds" were bunking for the winter months. Our yard looked like an amazing "tunnel" park. The children loved playing outside and would run through these shoveled paths like mice in a "maze." Only Emily Jane and Ryan did not panic as the mouse might have as they knew their way out and there were no deadly "traps" awaiting them.

Popcorn popped along with a fresh bowl of confectionary sugar made into frosting was a delicacy at our home and helped us soothe over the discomforts of the long, cold winter. When company came to our house, there would always be a large bowl or two of popcorn on the table. After scooping some frosting onto your plate, you then took one kernel of popcorn, dipped it into the frosting, and then back to your bowl of popcorn. This process would bring out a tongue-loving cluster of a delicious tasting goodie. These clusters became a delightful treat for all. It seemed there was never enough popcorn and I would have to make another batch. It might sound nauseating but try it and it will make you a believer!

Ryan had the most problems with the separation from his father. He loved his father and wanted to be with him. He was too young to understand even after I sat down with him and explained why his daddy was not living with us anymore. He should not have had to go through the anger he felt because of his parents mistakes. When he came home after visitations with his father, it took some time to assure him that he would be okay, that I loved him and wanted him to love his father, too. It was hard for him to process his father being with another woman and this created an even more colorful firecracker of emotions.

Emily Jane was older, saw reasons for the separation, and wanted to know why I did not leave Charlie sooner? She did not understand why Charlie was not a responsible father and why any woman would have to put up with his abuse and nonsense.

She was right. Why did I? Not wanting to admit I made a mistake in letting him move in with me or because I was hoping he would change were not good reasons for me to have stayed with him. The scars left by the four-way affair followed me wherever I went and they left me depleted of any self-value, and played a major part in choices I made in life. These scars led me to believe I did not deserve anything better especially with regards to relationships. Staying with Charlie is proof of this. He had just taken over the cycle of abuse where the four adults had left off. It produced the same degrading feelings and left me feeling worthless.

Our separation was smooth sailing and relatively uneventful until one gloomy, cloudy weekend. On this particular Saturday morning, Charlie came to pick up the children for their overnight visit with him. We had agreed he would bring them home by five o'clock on Sunday night. When Charlie did not return the children, I called his home to see if there was a problem and to find out when the children would be coming back. His new girlfriend told me that "they did not have to bring the children back as I did not have custody of them." So, they did not bring the children back. I was devastated.

At this point, we had been separated for over a year, and I had never had any problems trusting that Charlie would bring the children home when his visits with them were over. There was never any regular visitation established, and his actions surprised me as he never indicated that custody was something he would be interested in. Big mistake! Never just assume what the other person wants or is thinking! This was a hard lesson learned. With a lump still in my throat from the phone call the night before, I rose up early in the morning and was at the courthouse when the doors opened at 9:00 o'clock. I petitioned the court for temporary custody. Twenty-four hours later the children were back in my care.

As time passed, the children were thriving, accepting their newest situation, and enduring. We were making friends, and it seemed that we had guest for dinner every Saturday and Sunday nights. It was fun for all of us. I invited people who had children of their own. After our dinners, we would play games or watch a movie. Of course, we had our popcorn and frosting treat, too! I tried hard to make life enjoyable for Emily Jane and Ryan.

I did the best I could with what I had. The children would always know that I would be there for them. I also wanted them to have a relationship with their father, too. Charlie didn't seem to ever measure up to the father image we all hope our fathers to be. He would go for long periods without regular contact with his children. We all make mistakes, and, anyone can change if they really want to so I was still hopeful that they would be able to build a lasting relationship with their father. I was sad to see the children in the center of our situation. Breakups are damaging to all involved. There is nothing funny about them as depicted by some of the television shows being aired today.

Late in the fall, Charlie informed me that to avoid paying court ordered child support he was avidly thinking of ways he could get his children away from me and relieve him of his financial burden. He informed me that he was determined to pay me back for leaving him as I had. He would get even. One day, I had come home and found a business card on my front door. I had thought Ryan was with his father and Emily Jane was still at school. Wrong! They were not. At this time, they were in the hands of the Child Protection Services. I just about collapsed on my front doorsteps.

Once inside, I called the number on the card and learned I would be facing child abuse charges. Seriously? A court hearing had been set up and I would have to appear before a judge. I wanted to die. Charlie had promised me he would hurt me if I left him. Today, he had succeeded, with his evil plan. He really had a way of getting anything he wanted. Unbelievable!

During the time until the court hearing, I was not to have any contact with my children either in person or by telephone. I was devastated. I prayed to God for endurance, and close friends from my local Christian Congregation spent hours trying to comfort and support me through my trial. They were an invaluable source of love and support. I will admit that despite my prayers and the loving support I received, I really could not get my mind around the circumstances completely and I truly struggled emotionally. Flashbacks of the time when I was living at the 'white house' were jumping out at me, and I was remembering how Irene tried to take my brothers and sisters and me from the care of our mother. I remembered the fear and the anger I was feeling and how I did not want to be alive. I wanted to hurt myself or hurt someone. Today, I was feeling these emotions all over again.

I also received strong support from the case manager from Protective Services. It was clear to her that Charlie's accusations stemmed from his disliking the idea of financially contributing to raising his children. This brought my mind back to the time we were living in the 'two brown houses,' and Charlie received a court summons for child support of his other two children and there had been a similar outcome. I guess he was just going to make having children and leaving them without support a dirty, little habit forming way of life. I had underestimated this man capabilities and his new co-habitant was going to be in for some surprises of her own no doubt. Still, I would have to wait to settle this matter regarding the children in court. I did appear in court and after being interrogated and having a character witness take the stand in my behalf, it was determined that the charges against me were unfounded. Twenty-one long days after the children should have arrived home, they were coming home to me again. Thank God!

Emily Jane was testy at first but after a while, she fell back into her normal routine. She knew that what her father had done was cruel. Ryan, on the other hand, was inconsolable. Evidence of his anger and pain was seen in his eyes as he would stare at me. He was hurting. I was hurting for him. What Charlie and his future wife did hurt our family immeasurably. I did not think I could ever find it in my heart to be forgiving for what they had done to my children. Ryan was never the same.

I filed for a divorce, was awarded custody and exactly two months after our divorce, Charlie married for the third time. His new wife Nola had money. Charlie was having a field day. He was buying her jewelry and planning romantic getaways with her credit cards, traveling and living a life of ease. Nola eventually learned the hard way, unfortunately, who Charlie was and where his intentions came from. She and I came to understand each other very well many years down the road. I could sense that she truly loved the children and wanted what was best for them.

To his horror, Charlie was required to pay monthly child support. He was furious and fussed and fumed angrily for decades that he had been so punished by the outrageous court system. He honestly spent hours yelling at the children, I would later learn from them, cursing me and the fact that I had taken him to court and requested financial contribution. He never grasped the concept that he was the one who actually started the court procedure by alleging child abuse allegations and lies. Nola was sorry for this horrible slanderous experience later, but Charlie never even saw the connection that he went to court and was subsequently ordered minimal visitation and would have to pay monthly child support because of his abuse claims. Of all the years since that court order, what he paid me did not amount to more than five hundred dollars. This was less than the amount I should have gotten for two months of support. Charlie had told me that if I took him back to court to demand enforcement of payment, he would never see the children again. I opted not to press the support issue as I wanted the children to be able to see him. No amount of money on earth would be able to console the children later in life if they never had had a chance to know their father. Money was not worth seeing their pain in the future had they missed out in getting to know their father. I opted to do without and to allow them to see their father when he followed through with visitations.

We never really did go without. God was always with us, providing for our material, physical and emotional needs. I worked hard and we may not have had a Cadillac, but we did have a working car and eventually a brand new one. It was the cutest, gray Subaru. Imagine a new car! The children may not have had designer clothing to wear to school, but they had new clothes and they did not have to wear the same outfit every day for a whole year, as I had done when I went to school. I used my money wisely. Planning for the needs of the whole family was my priority. Any money left over meant we would have extra treats.

I will admit that I had made many mistakes as I raised my children, but I was never abusive. I know that I can look back on my time with both of my children and believe that I gave them my all. I gave them more than I could ever believe was possible. I did not play games with their minds. I did not hide my mistakes from them. I could say I was sorry and I did try harder to rectify my errors. I did not put wedges around them that would prevent them from becoming who they should be or who they wanted to be.

After the divorce was finalized, Charlie played his part to some degree. He boasted that he wanted his children to have what I could not give them. (Of course this was at Nola's expense.) He was always buying them clothing items and taking them places I never could afford to do so myself. He was always trying to buy their affection. They were able to see a little more of the world than I could have brought to them. Nola was free with her money and let Charlie use plenty of her money to give material things to his children that they otherwise would never have had. The children enjoyed these benefits and Emily Jane really became close to Nola. Ryan, however, did not connect with her or with Charlie. He liked the toys and candy, but was not happy about anything else. This was truly heartbreaking. Like many things Charlie attempted, it wasn't long before he was on to something new, and just began building another life with Nola, that didn't include his past or his children, and he began to take less and less of an interest in seeing them.

Reintegration and forming stability in our new life would take some time, love and effort, but we now had beautiful, country, idyllic surroundings to finally begin our journey as the nuclear family that we now legally were. For now the fresh country air would soothe our worn souls and we had the privilege of living in a home with a piece of paradise all around us that would console us while we worked at rebuilding our lives and preparing ourselves for anything we would have to face in the future. We were learning to relax and relish in the quiet peace of our serene conditions. I was learning to become the woman and mother I had longed to be. I was beginning a new way of living that was clean and non-toxic. I was developing relationships with integral people. I was learning the real meaning of love and light and how to live and thrive in these new environments. I knew this would be a healthier foundation for me to continue to raise my children.

I wished to mold my children as the mother I dreamt of being and provide for them a platform of honesty and integrity. Charlie faded into his own little world. He was busy traveling and shaking hands with crystal glasses and did not reach out often. This was more of a blessing than a curse because we were able to settle and adjust. I will always be grateful to my friends who offered me the opportunity of a lifetime when they opened their home to us, and the gratitude that filled my heart as we were to be able to lay our heads on a warm, indoor and cozy bed every night was overwhelming. I had journeyed over a long road of heartache and hardships, suffering and regrets, and had finally reached the other side. Thank God (literally)!

# MY RETURN
## (The Epilogue)

Thirty years would pass before I (Julianne) would return to scenic Massachusetts. Three decades of memories transpired before I saw anyone bound to me by blood relation. Of the four adults involved in the wife-swapping web only one remained living, my mother, Edith. My father, Gerard, the stocky woman, Irene and her husband David, had all passed on, leaving behind only miniscule traces of proof that they actually existed. They died lonely, unloved and for the most part their death robbed them of an opportunity to be forgiven by those of us who were still wearing the scars of our yesteryears. I often wished over the years that I would have been able to see them again and allow them to seek forgiveness.

Louisa had moved away with her family shortly after I had left the house at the bottom of the school hill and she, too, has strong feelings around the memories of her past. She is hoping that someday she will be able to put her thoughts down in writing for others to read. She is the mother I always knew she would be and evidence of this is reflected in the fact that both of her children grew up loved and protected allowing them to be who they were meant to be. Louisa truly blossomed into a wonderful, caring woman and our relationship now is how I always imagined one should have with her sister.

Gabriel lives alone and has his own routine. He keeps himself busy in his garden and taking care of his land while still enjoying his beers. He was not open to discussing the yesteryears and angrily exclaimed: "What good would it do? We can't change anything!" However, I didn't see it this way. Yes, it is true that we can't change what happened to us in the past but, there WAS still time to correct on going mistakes or make positive changes for the benefit of all those who are still ALIVE today. It would have to be a "team" effort. Gabriel declared to me that he was not interested in reuniting with me even after wondering for thirty years what had happened to me. Scars of his past weighed heavily on his soul and he was not interested in taking steps to work together as a family. He was not going to have any further discussions with me regarding the events of our past either. I really feel these could have gone far in soothing our wounds. His unwilling "team" spirit would not help our family move forward. This would be a real shame for all of us.

Alan had his own say about the family and the scars of his past. Evidence of the stresses he endured has shown themselves in the aches and pains he experiences today as he ages. He was very sickly as a child and it seems that the pattern of failing health never took a better path. He lives with his wife and children and has no interest in trying to do his part in reuniting with me or the family. This, too, is another real shame.

Chloe' passed away, but not before calling me to ask my forgiveness for the part she had in creating situations that had caused me pain and suffering while we were growing up. Happily, I was able to speak with her several times before she passed on. I was glad that we had the chance to set things right in our relationship. She thanked me for teaching her to play guitar and she let me know that music had played a major part in her life and it would continue 'til the day she died. Even though she had not reached certain educational and spiritual goals she had set for herself, Chloe' seemed content with many of the paths her life took. Not too long after we reconnected, Chloe' took her last breath of life. I was happy to know she died with a measurable amount of peace in her heart. I long for the time I will see her again.

Aude enjoyed the excitement of seeing me after all the lost years, but she did not enjoy the flashbacks that my presence brought back to her mind. Her pains and sorrows had held her back in life and she really never ventured too far away from home. It saddened me to note that she had never married or had children of her own as I had always thought she would have made a wonderful mother. Aude has so much love to offer to others. Still, though, she doesn't seem to have the courage or the energy to reach out so that she can share this love. Major depressed and suppressed emotions prevent her from even trying. It is difficult for me to see Aude face to face. Her own life's horrors are written all over her face and I can see the pain she is still harboring behind her eyes. Memories of all that she had to endure while we were growing up keep flashing like a continuing blinking light in my mind. All these years later, it is difficult for me to keep these memories in control and keep them where they belong—in the past. I know if this is hard for me to see, then I know it must be just as hard for Aude. They say a picture is worth a thousand words and I will say there are thousands of these words written on her face. They have never been erased. My heart bleeds for her and wishes she could move forward.

Mildred is a replica of our mother Edith only younger in years. She still has the glow of sunshine in her eyes when she smiles despite all that she has been through in her life. After marrying and leaving the area herself, she eventually returned to our hometown and lived with Aude for quite a while after her divorce. Later, she did manage to find a small place of her own where she could once again continue to spread her wings. Even though she personally had never been physically abused by Irene, Mildred does have her own share of stories to tell about what went on in our house when we were younger. If words of anger or ridicule spoken back then were bullets in a machine gun, then Mildred too has evidence of wounds that have not been addressed and dealt with in a healthy way.

Even though I had contacted my half-brothers and one of Irene and David's children since returning home, it seems like they, too, had their own way with dealing with our past. Most choose to block out the memories of the various abuses while others were trying to replace these memories with other interests. They were investing their time and energy on trying to move ahead. I have not had the opportunity to see any of them since my coming home nor have they shown any interest in seeing me.

Lastly, but not least, is my mother Edith. Upon seeing Edith in person after so many absentee years, I now had a chance to ask some of the questions that I had wanted answers to for almost half of my lifetime. I was willing and eager for both of us to have a fresh start, a do-over. I gave her the opportunity to ask for forgiveness and to see if there could be any hope for an honest relationship with me. Over and over again she did say she was sorry for what I/we had endured at the hands of the other three adults, but somehow she was thoroughly convinced in her mind (and tried in vain to convince me) that she was and had been a brilliant mother who gave her children every opportunity and was not a perpetuator of abuse. I spent many hours trying to reason with my mother and help her see the benefits of asking all her remaining, angry children for forgiveness and to try and build a relationship with a stronger foundation, one built on truth and love, before it was too late for her and them and for me. Sadly, Edith did not accept this offer and asked me to "please stop bringing up the past." She was finding it easier to keep her distance. Even though it appeared that she had little real interest in a true mother/daughter relationship I sensed that she was bluffing. I think she would have wanted one but there was something about the newness of this idea that might have had her running scared. Then, again, how could there be any kind of reconciliation when in her mind, all eleven children born (the total number of children from both families involved) had made up these horrible stories, accounts of abuse and accusations against her and her three cohorts. She even, to my utter disbelief, referred to Irene as her best girlfriend several times in our conversations and could not see why such a statement as this was so horrible for my ears to hear. After a while I determined that something was "missing" in my mother's genetic makeup, and this was evident in the choices she made and the things she allowed to happen to herself and her children.

Edith lives alone and, for the most part, her life now is void of friends or much family interaction. To some degree, dementia which is so common in the elderly keeps her safe in a world of "make believe." Not being able to formulate a true relationship with my mother proved to be a great disappointment for me.

It was discouraging for me to have returned home after all these years and find such a pitiful remnant of a family. I felt so blessed to have left home when I did since it afforded me an opportunity to have a much fuller life than I would have had if I had stayed behind. Leaving Massachusetts also took me far away from the dysfunction I grew up around. I wouldn't have to be part of it anymore and, for the most part, I locked these memories away.

The life experiences that I have revealed in the pages of this book have weighed heavily on my soul, and their memories have haunted me throughout most of my life. Although, writing this book was therapeutic for me, my real intention for invading my past was to find answers. I wanted to learn what went wrong with our family. I wanted to learn when the dysfunctional craziness began, and where it had stemmed from. I have come to realize that the emotional scars we all carry may make it impossible to ever be able to accomplish this new beginning. We might never truly reunite and be a family again like we were before the stocky woman walked up our driveway. All my life, it was, and it still is, my heart's desire and deepest wishes for us to be a family. They say time heals even the deepest wounds, so I guess I will have to wait and see what the passing of "more" time will alleviate. I will continue to try and move forward yet at the same time I will still try to find answers to some of the lingering and whispering questions that I still have about my parents, especially my Mother. I have overheard so many tidbits of long held secrets and I am always going to be digging through the layers.

# Special Acknowledgements and Thanks to:

My brilliant and amazing daughter, Ophelia, for her hours of dedication while editing and helping to define this book,

My son, Scott, who took me on roads I never thought I would travel that helped to teach me to be the better person I am today,

Andrea L., Paul G. and Erica H., for their timeless support and encouragement through all the evolving stages of this book,

My Mother, My Father, My Brothers and My Sisters,

And to the following incredible people who have contributed greatly to my life's journey:

James,
Rebecca H., Bill and Kay T., David and Susan S,
Dorval, Claire, Michele, Sue and John,
And Dave and Kim D.

Debbie for her long distance energy and incredible love during the development process and to her husband, Ingo, for his ingenious engineering capabilities and hours of patience,

Winter Tree Productions for oversight of the 'Book Baby' process from beginning to and hopefully, no end in sight

THE END

3/13

# DATE DUE

CPSIA information can be obtained at www.ICGtesting.com
Printed in the USA
LVOW131546060313

323026LV00002B/226/P

9 781478 718499